Dear Dad, Love Laurie

Also by
Susan Beth Pfeffer

Dear Dad, Love Laurie

Susan Beth Pfeffer

Illustrated by the author

AN
APPLE
PAPERBACK

SCHOLASTIC INC.
New York Toronto London Auckland Sydney

ISBN 0-590-41682-0

12 11 10 9 8 7 6 5 4 3 2 1   6   9/8 0 1 2 3 4/9

Printed in the U.S.A.   28

To my forty odd cousins

June 24

Dear Dad,
    Mom says I have to write to you at least once a week, now that you've moved so far away.
    I don't think that's fair.

Love,
Laurie

June 29

Dear Dad,
    Mom says that I have to write to you before I go to summer camp. I don't know what she expects me to write. School ended. Being in fifth grade was okay. I'm glad I'm going to be going to middle school next year. I guess summer camp will be okay. I had a good time there last year, even if you and Mom had just split up. In summer camp, maybe they won't make me write to you.

Love,
Laurie

Dear Dad,

It isn't fair. I was just getting ready to write to you when the counselor said we all had to write to our mothers. I said I was writing to my father instead, and the counselor (her name is Moira and she has three big pimples, one on each cheek and one in the middle of her chin) said she didn't care, I had to write to my mother too. I said it was my mother who made me write to my father, and Moira said she didn't care if the Queen of England made me write to my father; as long as I was sleeping in the Robin cabin, and she was the counselor, I was going to write to my mother.

So I had to stop the letter I was writing to you, and write a postcard to Mom instead.

I asked Mom before I left camp whether I had to write to you all summer long and she said yes, absolutely, the way she does. But I bet she didn't realize I was going to have to write to her too.

Darin Greenburg, (she's in the bunk next to mine and the reason her name is Darin is because her parents made it up. I think it's pretty) has parents who are still married, and she only has to write one postcard and they both get it. She says she likes writing letters. She said she'd write my letters for me if I'd pay her, but Mom didn't give me enough money.

Love,
Laurie

Dear Dad,

This weekend was parents' weekend, and Mom came up to visit. Lots of other kids got homesick when they saw their parents, but I didn't cry once.

Both of Darin Greenburg's parents came, but lots of the other kids only had one parent. Some kids had a mother and a stepfather, and a few had a mother and a stepfather and a stepmother and a father.

Darin told me she was jealous of the kids who had lots of extra parents. She said it's real hard when you're stuck with a mother and a father and they're still married. They make her do all her homework on time, and she doesn't get any extra presents or go interesting places during vacation (except her parents took her and her little brother to Disney World last year).

I liked it when you and Mom were still married, but I guess you did make me do my homework.

> Love,
> Laurie

Dear Dad,

Thank you for my package! ! ! I loved everything in it! ! ! ! How did you know I wanted a poster of

Ross Perlman? He's my absolute favorite. Moira said I could hang it up by my bunk just as long as I didn't use Scotch tape. But she had masking tape, so I used that instead. Everyone in my cabin loves Ross Perlman and they all think it's neat my father sent me the poster.

Darin Greenburg says the only thing she ever gets from her father is books. It's a good thing too. I already finished all the books I brought, so I've been swapping with her. Sometimes we read instead of going to archery. I hate archery.

I also loved all the fudge you sent, and I shared it with everyone just the way you told me to (you could practically see new pimples pop out on Moira), and the magazines (everyone read *Teen Dreamboat* at least twice), and I especially loved the map of Missouri.

"Why did your father send you a map of Missouri?" Darin asked.

"Because that's where he lives now, so I can see what the state looks like," I said right back.

Moira says she never met anybody who lived in Missouri, but she bets it's real boring there. I hope her teeth fall out from eating too much fudge.

> Love,
> Laurie

July 31

Dear Dad,

We had races in swimming today and I came in third twice and second once. And in archery, I hit a bull's-eye only it was in someone else's target.

Darin Greenburg says she's had enough of camp already and can't wait to go home, but I kind of like it. We're going to camp out this weekend, and have a bonfire and tell ghost stories and roast marshmallows. Moira says she knows a ghost story so scary none of us'll sleep that night, but I think she's making that up.

Jamie Reilly (she's in my cabin too) has been going to camp for years now and she says it always rains when you're going to have a camp-out. She says she was camping out once and it rained so hard the rain put the fire out. She says nothing tastes worse than wet marshmallows.

Does it rain a lot in Missouri?

Love,
Laurie

August 4

Dear Dad,

The camp-out was great. It didn't rain at all (well, just a little bit and that was after we were in our tents). Moira really did know a scary ghost story. It was all about this dead person who kept coming back to her old school to get revenge on her old teachers. Even Darin liked it.

We sang songs too and played dumb games like Grandmother's Trunk and we each got to say what was the scariest thing we'd ever seen. Darin said it was her baby brother when they brought him home from the hospital. She says he's less weird-looking now. Jamie whispered to me that Moira's pimples were the scariest thing she'd ever seen, but when her turn came, she just said her mother when she was mad.

The scariest thing I ever saw was our apartment after you moved out, but I didn't want to say that, so I said it was Great-uncle Herbie the time he got all red at the wedding and had a heart attack and everybody thought he was going to die. That took third prize. Jennifer Hughes came in second with her father's third wife. Lisa Frolich won, but I'm not sure it's fair. The scariest thing she ever saw was a big truck that hit the car she and her mother were in. Her mother was in the hospital for months. The reason I don't think it's fair is because she was only a year and a half old then and I bet she doesn't really remember what the truck looked like.

I remember Great-uncle Herbie, though. Boy, was he red!

Love,
Laurie

August 10

Dear Dad,

Mom was here again this weekend for the second parents' weekend. She said she never gets any letters from me.

I said that's because you make me write letters to Dad, so all I write to you are the postcards Moira makes us all write.

Mom said that made sense to her.

Sometimes I really love her.

Love,
Laurie

Dear Dad,

Camp ends on Saturday. I'm really sad. I've been having a good time. I even like Moira. And Darin and Jamie and I have gotten to be such good friends that I can't believe I'm not going to see them again.

Darin said I could visit her over Thanksgiving. She says her mother makes a turkey and they have lots of people over, but I said I'd be spending Thanksgiving with you in Missouri. Jamie spends Thanksgiving with her father and stepmother. She says she misses having Thanksgiving with her mother, but she has Christmas with her and New Year's with her dad. Then she has her birthday with her mother and Easter with her father. Darin says she's stuck with both parents all the time, but sometimes I think she says stuff like that because she knows we're jealous of her. Jamie hates her stepmother and she has two stepbrothers and she says they're really mean.

Our cabin played the Bluebird cabin in softball

yesterday and we won 11–10. The Bluebirds thought they should have won but the umpire called two of their runners out when they tried to score so we won instead. I was up seven times and I got three hits and a walk and I struck out twice and grounded out once. One of my hits was a triple.

Lisa Frolich got hit by a pitch and she's still black-and-blue. She says if she isn't back to normal by the time school starts, she's going to sue the camp for millions of dollars. Her mother sued the truck-driver who hit her for millions of dollars and that's why they're rich now, but she says her mother's back hurts all the time and it would be nicer not to be rich and not to be in pain. She says her mother really hurts when it rains.

Darin says her grandmother can tell when it's going to rain because her rheumatism acts up.

Lots of times we talk after lights are out. We're supposed to whisper so we don't bother anybody else. But sometimes Moira gets interested in what we're talking about and then we all talk when we're not supposed to.

Oh yeah. Darin and Jamie both say that I write longer letters than anybody they've ever met and you must be really nice sending me that poster and everything and they wish they could meet you some-time. Only I guess they won't, if you live in Missouri.

You'd like them too, so maybe you should move closer to us.

Love,
Laurie

Dear Dad,

I got home from camp perfectly safe and Mom let me call Darin to make sure she got home too. She did. Then Mom took me out for a special welcome-home supper. I got a prime rib.

Mom said I shouldn't eat too much red meat, but I told her I hadn't been, that at camp all we ever ate were hot dogs and everybody at camp said they were made out of mouse intestines.

Mom turned kind of green then and she ended up changing her order and getting some kind of pasta with vegetables. She even threatened to make both of us vegetarians, but I think she's kidding.

Anyway, since all she'd had for supper was pasta and vegetables, Mom insisted we both have big goppy desserts. I got a hot fudge sundae, and Mom got a brownie with ice cream and whipped cream. She said we'd have to get back to normal tomorrow, but that was yesterday and we had pancakes for breakfast this morning.

She says it's because she missed me when I was at camp.

I missed her too, but now that I'm back home I don't miss her anymore, but I still miss you. And I miss Darin and Jamie. I even miss Lisa Frolich and I didn't like her very much.

Love,
Laurie

Dear Dad,

Kris Chandler came to visit me yesterday. I hadn't seen her since June.

She spent the summer mostly visiting her grandparents. They have a farm in Indiana and she likes spending the summer there. They have cows and chickens and pigs and ducks. She says chickens are terrible, but she likes the ducks.

I told her all about camp and Darin and Jamie and I showed her my Ross Perlman poster (which I hung up by the side of my bed so he's the first thing I see when I wake up in the morning. Mom said I could use Scotch tape). She loved the poster. I told her you sent it to me and she said you were always the nicest father she knew except hers and he never even heard of Ross Perlman. I think you're nicer than Mr. Chandler. He shouted at me once when I was visiting Kris because I talked during a third-down-and-two play, but everybody in the stands was screaming, so I don't see what difference it makes that I talked. I wasn't even there, just watching the game on TV. I didn't tell Kris you were nicer though because maybe you shouted at her once and I just don't remember.

It's been really hot here, much hotter than it was at camp. Mom sweats all the time. The living room air conditioner is just kind of working. Mom says if it would really break she could complain to the landlord about it, but as long as it makes lots of noise and a little bit of cold air, she doesn't think the landlord would care. So we don't spend much time in the living room.

I asked her if it was hot in Missouri and she said it's always hot in Missouri. Is that true?

Love,
Laurie

September 3

Dear Dad,

School starts next week, but Mom went in today to look at her classroom. She says she always cries at the start of each new school year, and then she cries when the school year ends. She says she cries lots of times during the school year too, but she'd still rather be a teacher than anything else.

She says you must be real busy, now that you're an assistant superintendent of schools and that's why you haven't written back to me to tell me if it's hot in Missouri. She says you'll write as soon as you have the chance, but meanwhile I have to keep writing to you.

I almost don't mind writing letters to you, but I like it when you write back. And just because I'm home doesn't mean you can't keep sending me packages. Mom says no fudge, but posters and books and other junk is fine with her. She was sorry I didn't bring back my copy of *Teen Dreamboat*. She says it's real useful knowing who the teen dreamboats are nowadays. I don't know why she has to know that stuff, but she says sometimes her students mention someone, and it helps if she knows who the person is.

I think it's real exciting going to a brand-new school. I was getting pretty tired of elementary school. Now I'll be in middle school for three years, and then I'll be in the high school.

Kris says it kind of scares her starting a new school, but we figure as long as we have each other and Shannon and Maria and even Jimmy, we should be okay. Jimmy used to be almost my best friend after Kris, but last year he started acting weird, and Mom says that kind of stuff only gets worse in sixth grade. She says first they act weird and then they start shaving and then the next thing you know they're taking you to the senior prom.

I don't think I want to go to the senior prom with Jimmy but I guess I have seven years to make up my mind. Kris says she wants to go to the senior prom with Ross Perlman, but I bet he doesn't ask her.

Love,
Laurie

September 10

Dear Dad,

Guess what! I am now a genuine middle school student. I started Dale Baker Middle School yesterday, and today was the first full day of school.

It rained so hard this morning Mom thought maybe there was a hurricane and we wouldn't have school at all, but the bus came just like it was supposed to, only we all got wet waiting for it.

Mom says I should tell you what classes I'm taking and who my teachers are. I have Mr. Rodriguez for reading (I think he's cute, but Kris doesn't like his mustache), and Ms. Oslow for math, and Mr. Brown for social studies, and Mrs. Larue for science. In social studies we're going to study all the different states, and we each have to write a report on one, so I asked if I could do Missouri. Mr. Brown said almost nobody ever volunteered to do Missouri so I explained you were living there now. So then Amy Yagoda said she wanted to do Missouri too, but it turned out she meant Mississippi. Her parents got arrested there once, and they talk about it a lot.

I like Mr. Brown and Mrs. Larue seems okay, but I don't think I'm going to like Ms. Oslow. She said she was sure we'd all forgotten all our arithmetic over the summer and we were going to spend this week doing nothing but the times tables which is baby stuff. I remember that seven times eight is fifty-six (or is it fifty-four?). Fifty-six. See. I remembered.

Mr. Rodriguez said if our class read enough books then Burger Bliss would treat us all to hamburgers, but it wouldn't be fair if two kids read twenty books each, and everybody else read just one, so we'd all have to read a lot because he hated to turn down a free meal. And Mrs. Larue said we'd study the planets and the stars and gravity. We'll each get to do a planet, but I don't know which one I want yet. It would be easier if you lived on one, like Jupiter or Pluto, the way you live in Missouri.

Kris is in all my classes with me and so's Shannon and Jimmy, but Maria is in different classes and when we saw her at lunch, she cried. Shannon and Maria have always been in the same class, and Shannon's pretty upset too. It's scary being in a new school, but if you have your best friend with you, it makes it feel okay. Poor Maria is in the same class with Gracie Schultz, and they've always hated each other. Mom says sometimes you start out in sixth grade hating someone and by the time the year ends, you're best friends, but I don't think Maria and Gracie are ever going to be best friends.

Also I have gym and two days a week I have music and two days a week I have art and one day a week I have home ec (Mom says she can't wait until I learn how to cook so we can eat better), and I have French too! Our teacher is Mrs. Hulbert, but we have to call her Madame. And lunch.

There's a school band, and Mom says I can be in it if I want, but I have to be willing to practice, so I don't think I'll join. I'm pretty tired of playing the bassoon.

Love,
Laurie

September 14

Dear Dad,
In school today on the loudspeaker they told a bunch of kids to go to the principal's office, and

Kris was one of the kids they named. Kris didn't know what was going on, since she never did anything bad, but she told me later they asked her and maybe twenty other kids from the sixth grade if they wanted to be part of the school's gifted and talented program.

Kris says it means lots of extra work for her, doing stuff like science projects, but they'll go on special trips and get to meet interesting people and she's really excited she got picked.

I don't understand why I didn't get picked. I'm just as gifted and talented as she is. I even told her so. I said "I play the bassoon and I write stories and draw pictures and buy great gifts for people." Don't I, Dad? Remember a couple of years ago when I got you that book about baseball cards? That was my idea and you loved it.

Kris said she didn't think gifted meant you bought great gifts and I hadn't played the bassoon in months, and didn't like playing it much when I did, which I don't think is the point at all. I did used to play it after all, and Mr. Fitzpatrick said I was a good bassoonist. And I write much better stories than Kris and besides, she doesn't know her left from her right. She's always getting them mixed up, and she's in sixth grade already, same as me. I learned my lefts from my rights before first grade even, and Kris still has to ask me sometimes which one's which. So I've got to be at least as gifted and talented as she is if not more so.

Then after Mom got home from school we had a big fight about it. I told her how mad I was that Kris was gifted and talented and I wasn't, and she said Kris always did better academically than I did, like that has anything to do with being gifted and talented. Sure, Kris's grades are better than mine are, but they wouldn't be if they tested her on lefts and rights all the time. She'd still be in kindergarten if they did that. And my grades used to be as good as Kris's until you and Mom got divorced and I read in one of Mom's books that lots of times kids' grades go down when there's a divorce. So it's practically Mom's fault I'm not in the gifted and talented program, and I kind of told her that, and that's when she got mad. Actually she got really mad when I said that since it was all her fault, she should talk to everybody in the middle school to get me into the gifted and talented program. She is a teacher in the school district, after all, and you used to be an assistant principal at the high school.

You know how red Mom's face used to get when she was screaming at you? That's what she looked like, almost as red as Great-uncle Herbie. She said she thought there was nothing worse than when a parent used her influence to get her kid into some kind of special program, and she would never do that, and if I didn't earn something on my own, it didn't count anyway, and she didn't see what I was making such a big fuss about. She said if Kris hadn't been accepted into the gifted and talented program, then I wouldn't care, and all I was was jealous, but that isn't true. I belong in the program because I can draw and play the bassoon and know my lefts from my rights. So I want you to write a letter to everybody in the middle school and ask them to put me in the gifted and talented program, fast, before I miss anything, and Kris gets to lord it over me that she did something great and I didn't. And if you do that, it'll make up for the way my grades went down because you and Mom got a divorce.

Love,
Laurie

P.S. You don't have to tell Mom when you write the letters.

September 19

Dear Dad,

This has definitely been the worst week of my life in years. First Kris was accepted in the gifted and talented program and I wasn't and Mom got mad at me. Then the next day I had an awful stomachache, and Mom didn't believe me, and made me go to school, and I threw up during French class, and I practically didn't make it to the bathroom on time, because we're only supposed to talk in French, and I didn't know how to say "Excuse me please but I'm about to throw up." Madame Hulbert made an announcement after I got back that if any of us thought we were going to throw up, we could just say it in English, fast, and everybody laughed, except me. I wanted to cry. So then the nurse wanted to send me home, but Mom was working, and I had to spend the rest of the day in the nurse's office just in case I threw up again, which I almost did twice, and everybody kept peeking in on me, and the nurse asked me if I knew about menstruation, which I did, but I didn't think it had anything to do with throwing up.

So Wednesday, Mom let me stay home from school, even though I pretty much felt okay, but I guess she figured I might start throwing up again, and I bet Madame Hulbert was relieved I wasn't there. I watched all the TV shows Mom won't let me watch, but mostly I was bored. That proved to me what a gifted and talented person I was. Other people would want to stay home from school, but us gifted and talented people want to learn all the time. Except during math. I really don't like Ms. Oslow. She shouts at us all the time and gives too much homework. But I bet most gifted and talented people don't like math either.

Then Thursday I went back to school, and I was talking to Shannon (she isn't in the gifted and talented program either, but she doesn't seem to mind) and I mentioned that I really liked going to Dale Baker, and some eighth-grader who was walking by sneered at me and said, "Everybody knows you only call it Baker." He made me sound like such a baby. I've only been at school two weeks, and they've practically been the worst two weeks of my life, so I don't see how I'm supposed to know you only call it Baker. It isn't like any of our teachers taught us that.

And then on Friday I had three surprise quizzes. I think all the teachers ganged up to see how they could make us the most miserable, and they decided to all give us surprise quizzes. It worked too. By the last quiz, I was ready to cry all over again.

Then today Kris was supposed to come over, only she had to cancel because she had a big gifted and talented meeting, where the parents were supposed to go and hear all the wonderful things their kids were going to get to do. And then Mom told me to stop pouting, and I guess I kind of shouted at her, and she yelled back, and then she said I should write you a letter, even though I wrote you less than a week ago.

"Let him share in the parenting experience," is what she said. So I'm writing you this letter.

I miss you because you never shouted at me.

Love,
Laurie

September 20

Dear Dad,

I told Mom I wrote you a letter and that I missed you because you never shouted at me, and she laughed, but not like she thought it was funny. She says you did your share of shouting.

I think sometimes Mom wishes she could have divorced me right along with you.

Love,
Laurie

Dear Dad,

I'm in my bedroom, and Mom just knocked on my door, and asked me if I'd written to you this week. So I said sort of because I wrote you on Sunday, but she said I should write today, because tomorrow we're going to drive to Gran and Grandpa's to spend the day with them. So that's why I'm writing. Besides, she said good stuff happened to me this week, and you'd probably like getting a letter where I told you good things. So I said I always told you good things in my letters, and she said fine, she just thought you'd enjoy hearing even more.

So here are the good things.

I got back my three surprise quizzes and I got a 92, and an 88 and a 100! The 100 was in science, where we're studying the solar system. I really like astronomy. Right now, my favorite planet is Venus, but I think I'm going to do my report on Neptune. Everyone else wants to do their report on Venus or Mars, and I feel kind of sorry for Neptune. It's so big and nobody cares about it.

The 88 was in math, but this week we had a scheduled test, so I got to study, and I got a 90 in it. And the 92 was in social studies. I forgot two state capitals, or else I would have gotten a 100 in that too.

Kris came over after school on Wednesday and stayed for supper. Mom bought us a pizza with mushrooms and onions and extra cheese and we all ate it together on the living room floor. Mom said pizza tastes best on floors. Kris said her mother never let her eat on floors, and Mom said her mother never did either, which I thought was pretty funny, because her mother is Gran, and I can't picture Gran doing anything on a floor except walking. Or standing. And last night Mom and I went to the movies together. We saw *Grateful Ghosts,* rated PG. We both thought it was really funny. So I guess I love Mom after all.

I just went into the living room and told Mom that I wrote that I loved her to you. She smiled. So I asked her if she loved me and she said yes, absolutely, and I asked if she loved me all the time, even when I was throwing up or complaining, and she said yes, absolutely again. I kind of figured she did, but there was no harm asking.

Do you love me all the time too?

Love,
Laurie

September 30

Dear Dad,

I never before in my life got a telegram and I love it! It's the most wonderful thing I ever saw! At first I wasn't sure why you sent me one that said "Yes, absolutely," but then I realized you were answering my question about if you loved me all the time. So I told Mom, because she was wondering too, and she hugged me, and said, "You're a lucky girl, Laura

Diane Levine, and you write to your father and tell him just how much you love him too."
I love you a million billion tons.

Love, love, love, love, love,
Laurie

P.S. Don't worry. I'll write you a real letter soon.

October 4

Dear Dad,
Except for your telegram, which I told everybody about and they were all so jealous, especially Kris, who said her father would never send her a telegram because they live under the same roof, this has been a very boring week. All I did was go to school and do my homework and watch TV. Tuesday is Yom Kippur, and Mom says I can fast if I want to. Maybe that'll be interesting.
I'd write to you more, except it's all so BORING and besides, if you put this together with the thank you letter I wrote, it's just about a complete letter.

Love,
Laurie

Dear Dad,

There wasn't any school yesterday because it was Yom Kippur and I fasted the whole day. Mom and I went to Temple, which went on forever, but the fasting was interesting. My stomach rumbled a lot, especially around lunchtime and around two in the afternoon I got light-headed and wanted to giggle, only Mom wouldn't let me because everybody was praying. She said I could eat if I wanted, but I didn't want to.

I thought the day would never end, but eventually they blew the shofar and we all got to go home and eat, and after Mom called Gran and Grandpa to make sure they were okay, she told me I could call Darin Greenburg, from summer camp, because Kris and Shannon and Maria aren't Jewish. Guess what? Darin fasted too, and it was the first time she ever fasted, and she did giggle from two-thirty until practically three. Isn't that amazing? Sometimes I think Darin would be my absolute best friend except she doesn't live nearby.

So I told Darin all about my friends here, and she said Kris might be in the gifted and talented program, but she bet she never fasted, which is true, because I asked Kris on Monday and she said she certainly never had. She didn't even think her parents would let her if she wanted to. They worry that she doesn't eat enough, and when she spent the summer in Indiana, she says her grandparents made her eat double portions of everything because she's so skinny.

Kris is doing her social studies project on Indiana, which she says is a very interesting state, and I'm doing mine on Missouri. She has a real advantage, because she's been to Indiana, which I pointed out to Mom is just the kind of reason why Kris got picked for the gifted and talented program and I didn't. Mom said I'd be going to Missouri for Thanksgiving and I could take a camera with me so I could take lots of pictures of Missouri for my report. So I asked Mom if I could take a camera to Neptune when I do my report on it and Mom laughed. She said I was a gifted and talented comedian.

Kris is doing her report on comets. I think that's kind of show-offy, but Mrs. Larue said comets were part of our solar system, so she could. Shannon's going to do Pluto. She says Pluto should be the easiest one because nobody knows anything about it, so she shouldn't have to read too much.

Did you fast on Yom Kippur? Mom says she bets you forgot to. Mom also says we can call Nana and Gramps down in Florida this weekend, so I can tell them I fasted. She says they'll be proud of me.

I can't wait to tell Kris how hungry I got. I bet she's never been that hungry before in her life.

Love,
Laurie

October 10

Dear Dad,

We called Nana and Gramps this morning and I told them I fasted, and they said I was such a big girl now. Almost eleven, I said. Nana said she didn't fast for the first time until she was twelve, but Gramps said kids got mature faster now because of vitamins and cable TV.

So then I told them I'd be going to Missouri for Thanksgiving, and Nana said why didn't I go to Florida over winter vacation and visit with them there, and you could fly in from Missouri and we could all have some time together. I was on the phone in Mom's room, and Mom was on the kitchen phone, but I could hear her thinking about it, and then she said, "Yes, absolutely, I should have thought of that myself," and Nana said she was a pearl and her son was a jackass for letting her get away.

I think that kind of embarrassed Mom because she changed the subject right away to how I was doing in school. So I told them about the projects I was going to be doing, and the books I was reading, and how I hated Ms. Oslow, but I was still getting 90s in math, and Gramps said I was certainly the smartest granddaughter he had, but he can say that because Uncle Mike has two sons so I'm the only granddaughter he has. Of course Larry and Kenny aren't that smart, so I'm probably the smartest grandchild he has, but I figured I'd better not say it, so I didn't. Mom didn't either, but I guess now that she's divorced she has to be polite about that sort of thing.

Anyway, Mom said she'd talk to you about Florida, and Nana said she'd talk to you about Florida, but I figured I'd write to you about Florida first. I think it's the most wonderful idea I ever heard of. Kris is going to Indiana for winter vacation, and she says it always snows there, and it's real pretty, but cold. Nana said I could go swimming in Florida. She said that's why people retire to Florida and not Indiana.

So then Gramps said he wanted to watch the baseball game, and Nana sent me a thousand kisses and we got off the phone. And now I'm writing to you. Don't plan anything else for winter vacation, okay? You and me and Nana and Gramps and Florida will be perfect!

Love,
Laurie

P.S. I don't really think Nana thinks you're a jackass. I'd ask Mom, but I have a feeling that wouldn't be a smart question.

October 15

Dear Dad,

Guess what? Mom and I were having supper (chicken, and rice, and green beans. Mom says I should tell you what I'm eating so you won't worry), and it's Thursday, which is always Mom's absolute worst day, but she said because she got Monday off, she was in a pretty good mood. So then she said, "You know you have a birthday coming up." As though I didn't know. So I said, "Yes, on October 30, which is two weeks from tomorrow, and I can't wait, because I'm so bored with being ten, and practically everybody I know is eleven already." They all are too. Kris has been eleven for five months now, which is why she got into the gifted and talented program and I didn't. They probably said, "We can't have any ten-year-old babies in our gifted and talented program no matter how gifted and talented they are." I haven't told Kris that, but that's what I think.

So Mom said, "The day after your birthday is Halloween, and you can either have a Halloween party and invite ten kids from your class, or you can have a sleepover and invite Kris and Shannon and Maria and Darin and Jamie from summer camp." So I said, "Boys and girls at the Halloween party?" and Mom said yes.

So I thought about it. Last Sunday I went to Tara O'Shea's eleventh birthday party, and it was boys and girls and the boys acted really stupid. Joe Malone said he was king of all the boys and any boy caught talking with a girl would have to be punished and Ronny Petrocelli said that wasn't fair, he might want to kiss one of the girls, and Joe said that was okay because kissing wasn't talking, and I thought that was really mean, but Tara just giggled and Ronny walked right over and kissed her and she only giggled harder, and then Mark Klein said Ronny kissing Tara made him sick and he pretended like he was puking, and then all the boys did, and then Tara hit Mark and said boys were stupid and girls were smart and made all us girls go into her bedroom and close the door and pretend like the boys weren't there.

I don't think we could manage that in this apartment — boys in the living room, while the girls hide in my bedroom — and I know Mom wouldn't like it, so I decided to have the sleepover. Besides, I haven't seen Darin and Jamie since summer camp ended, and I want them to meet Kris and Shannon and Maria, who are my best friends ever, even Maria, who I never see anymore, because we're in all different classes. So Mom said I could call Darin and Jamie this weekend to invite them and everybody should bring sleeping bags and costumes and we'd tell ghost stories and try on makeup. She says that's what she did for her eleventh birthday except without the costumes because her birthday's in March. She also said we could go trick-or-treating around the apartment complex.

So I asked her if I could ask you to send a package, like you sent at summer camp, which was so perfect, and Mom said I could, but there probably wasn't any reason for you to send fudge, since we'd all be trick-or-treating. Then she said she wouldn't be trick-or-treating, and she's been jealous of me for three months now, getting that fudge in the mail, so you should send it if you don't mind her eating most of it. She says with walnuts please, because she likes to think it has less calories that way.

I think this is going to be the greatest-ever birthday party. I only wish you could be there, because you never met Darin or Jamie and they never met you, but Mom said Missouri is two car rides and two plane rides away from here, and besides men don't belong at sleepovers. She says they never know how to put makeup on right.

Love,
Laurie

P.S. I asked Mom if you'd know that sending a package with fudge isn't the same as sending a birthday present, and Mom said you were pretty smart about that kind of thing but if I was really worried, I should tell you. Ordinarily, the package would be just perfect for a birthday present, but the way Mom's been talking about that fudge, I don't think I'm going to get to even taste it, and I don't think it would be fair if my birthday present ended up in Mom's stomach, especially since the two of you are divorced.

Mom says if you're not sure what you should send me for my birthday, you should call her a week from Saturday in the afternoon, because I'm going to be at Jimmy's house then for his birthday party, and she can discuss gifts with you. But if you already know what you're getting me, then you shouldn't bother.

In case you need some ideas, I'd love a Walkman and my own phone and any new books by Judy Blume and Ellen Conford and Paula Danziger and a pink bedspread and all the *Star Wars* video cassettes. Also please convince Mom to let me get my ears pierced. All my friends have pierced ears, and I feel like such a baby because I don't.

I could also use a new bike.

P.P.S. I bet that was the longest P.S. in history!

Dear Dad,

Mom says I should write to tell you I got a 100 on my social studies test and a Very Good Plus on my book report. So I asked her if I should tell you about the 76 I got on my math test, and she said, "Sure, but start with the 100."

So I did.

Love,
Laurie

P.S. Don't forget to call Mom on Saturday if you need any ideas for presents. And everybody I invited to my birthday party is coming!

October 25

Dear Dad,

Yesterday was Jimmy's birthday party, and I asked Mom when I got back if you'd called her about presents, but she refused to answer, which I think is pretty mean of her. I did give you that list, but some things on it I wanted more than others, and besides, how can you convince her to let me get my ears pierced if the two of you don't talk? Having long-distance divorced parents makes my life very complicated.

Jimmy's party was terrible. It was like Tara's only worse because the other boys picked on Jimmy, which was really unfair because it was his birthday. There were eleven of us, six girls and five boys, and Joe Malone was one of the boys, which I don't understand at all, because he and Jimmy have never been friends. If I were only having eleven people at my birthday party, they'd all be my closest most personal friends, and not people like Joe Malone who think they know everything and are really very stupid. Jimmy's parents split up a few months ago, and his mother's at the stage where she cries all the time, so she kept saying, "My baby is eleven," and crying, and his big sister kept saying, "Do I have to stay here any longer?" which isn't the kind of thing that makes you have a good time at a party anyway. Then no one liked the games Jimmy's mother made us play, because they were baby games like Pin the Tail on the Donkey and Simon Says, and Joe said nasty things to Jimmy's mother and she cried some more.

Then Jimmy got to talking with me and Kris, and Joe and the other boys came over to him and called him a queer because he liked girls more than boys. So then Jimmy got mad and said queers didn't like girls, they only liked boys, so he guessed Joe was the biggest queer of them all. Joe hit Jimmy then, punched him right in the nose, and it started bleeding, and Kris and I were kicking Joe, and Michael Ricci, who's Joe's best friend, was pushing us and Jimmy's mother kept crying, and his big sister said, "You are all the most disgusting creatures I have ever seen." A couple of the other girls were crying by then, but Kris and I were too mad, and we kept kicking and pushing, and finally Jimmy's mother called all the other mothers, and we all went home early. So maybe you tried calling while Mom was picking me up.

I'm not sure I really know what a queer is, but I'm pretty sure Jimmy isn't one. I asked Mom about it, and she said a queer was a nasty word for a man who falls in love with other men, which doesn't make any sense to me at all. I can see being friends with other men but why should you fall in love with them if you already are one? Do you know anybody like that? Mom says she does, but she refused to tell me who. She said it was none of my business. She also said Joe Malone is the nastiest boy she knows, and Jimmy's mother should stop crying already. And I told her I was glad I was only having girls at my party, and she said she was glad too, and if she complained once about how much work it was, I should remind her about Jimmy's party, and she would shut right up.

I only wish I had something like that for the whole year. A mother-shutter-upper would be a great invention.

Mom also says to tell you that you don't really have to send me fudge for her to eat, that she's perfectly capable of getting fat on her own without any help from you, but that if you do send me fudge for her to eat, could you make it an assortment, with walnuts and without, and peanut butter and maple and everything else they have in fudge because she would never buy that stuff for herself, or me either, and the only way she'll ever eat it is if you do. She also says if there's an assortment, then she's more likely just to take a little piece of this

kind and a little piece of that, but I think she's
kidding herself, and will eat it all up and I won't
get any, so please send a double box-worth just so
I can get a taste.

Love,
Laurie

October 29

Dear Dad,

I love you so much and your package came today,
and I loved everything in it, and Mom says you sent
birthday presents too, but she won't give them to
me until my actual birthday tomorrow. So I guess
I'll have to write you again. But meantime, I love
my package. It was so great! I loved the magazines,
and the dinosaur-shaped water pistols (Mom says
she could have lived without those) and all that
fudge! I never knew there were that many kinds of
fudge in the world, and you sent so much that
there's enough for Kris and Maria and Shannon and
Darin and Jamie and me with tons left over for
Mom, who's already eaten two full pieces and says
thank you very much.

But the best thing was the videotape. I don't believe you did that, it was so wonderful of you. I
can't wait to show it to everybody Saturday night,
especially Darin and Jamie, because they never met
you. When they see you on the TV introducing
yourself, and telling that ghost story (I only listened

33

to the very beginning myself, so I could be scared by it along with everybody else), they'll know I have the best father in the whole world, which is what I've been telling them anyway. I think Mom said that sending that videotape was an extremely smart thing for you to do, but she had her mouth filled with rocky road fudge at the time so it was hard to understand.

You are the very best father in the whole world, and no matter what you got me for my birthday, even if it was just something dumb like underwear, I will love you forever and ever and promise to get great grades and be a lawyer or a doctor or both so you'll be proud of me when you're old.

                              Love,
                              Laurie

                    October 30 (my 11th birthday! ! !)

Dear Dad,
You are the best father who ever lived and I love my birthday presents, even though Mom said you spent far too much money, and she doesn't like the idea of you competing with her by buying expensive gifts. I think it's great and I love every single thing you sent me.

Here are my favorites:

The *Star Wars* video (and the promise of *The Empire Strikes Back* for Chanukah).

The new Ellen Conford book (which I'll read on Sunday, after everybody leaves).

And my super favorite — the pierced earrings!

Pearls! Now Mom has to let me get my ears pierced, so I can wear them. I begged her and begged her but until there actually were earrings, she kept saying no. Once I opened your presents, and there they were, she sighed a lot and then she said, "All right, we'll get them pierced tomorrow before everybody comes, just as long as you don't insist on getting your nose pierced later on."

You are the smartest father in the universe!

Mom gave me some books, and a sweater, and the pink bedspread I wanted, and a polar bear teddy bear which I named Jonathan. He's so cute, and he looks wonderful on top of my pink bedspread — he really stands out because he's bright white. Mom says she bought him so the next time the air conditioning doesn't work, we can look at him and pretend we're on the North Pole.

Gran and Grandpa sent me a really pretty doll (even though I'm kind of too old for that sort of thing) and Nana and Gramps sent me a whole box of seashell things, seashell stationery, and a seashell T-shirt, and seashell sheets (that look real pretty with the pink bedspread) and a poster that shows all the different kinds of seashells and what they come from. I'm going to put that right next to my Ross Perlman poster, so I can look at it first thing in the morning too. And in school today, everybody wished me a happy birthday, even Jimmy whose face gets kind of green lately whenever birthdays get mentioned. And Madame Hulbert had the whole class sing "Happy Birthday" in French to me. She does that every time one of us has a birthday, but it still made me feel special and kind of European.

Oh and Uncle Mike and Aunt Linda sent me this beautiful dress, real fancy, and on my birthday card Aunt Linda wrote that she hoped I didn't mind, but since she doesn't have a daughter, whenever she sees something pretty, she wants to get it for me, so this time she did. I tried it on and it fits me perfectly, and Mom says if I'm ever invited to a wedding or a coronation, I'll have the perfect occasion to wear it.

Tomorrow I'm having my real birthday cake, but since today was my birthday, Mom got us an ice-cream-cake roll and put a candle in it, and sang me "Happy Birthday" and we each had a piece. Ice-cream-cake roll is practically my favorite thing in the world to eat and she also got us Chinese take-out, and I got to have spareribs and eggplant with garlic sauce and egg rolls and chicken with cashews, which are all my favorite things (Mom usually makes me pick between the spareribs and the egg rolls). Also won ton soup, and my fortune cookie said, "This will be a rich and prosperous year for you." Honest. Mom's said "A little weight gained is a lot of weight to lose," so she had an extra piece of fudge with the ice-cream-cake roll.

I asked Mom if I blew out the candle on my cake tonight and blew out the candles on my cake tomorrow, whether I could make two wishes, or had to wish the same thing twice, and she said I could either make the two wishes, or have double strength on the one wish, so I'd better think hard about which I'd rather have. I decided to go with the two wishes because when I study for a test, I can get an 85, but when I study twice as hard, maybe I'll get a 95 or even a 100, but I won't get a 170. I told

Mom that and she said it was frightening how logical I'd gotten since I turned eleven.

I can't tell you what I wished for, but you were in my wish. And it didn't have anything to do with your sending me anything.

Tomorrow's my Halloween birthday sleepover and I know I'm going to have the best time ever and so will all my friends. Mom and I figure I'll probably want to write to you again on Sunday, to let you know how everything went, but I wanted to write to you before then to thank you again and again and again for my presents and to tell you I love being eleven and as soon as I wear your earrings, I'll get my picture taken so you can see how beautiful they are.

Love,
Laurie

P.S. I guess I'm the happiest person in the world right now. I've got to be the happiest eleven-year-old.
P.P.S. Does it make you feel old having an eleven-year-old daughter? Mom says nothing makes her feel old now that she dyes her gray hair, but after she thought about it, she ate another piece of fudge.

November 1

Dear Dad,

I am the most miserable person in the world, and I hate everybody and everything and life is so unfair and I wish I was dead.

Mom says I should write and tell you all about

37

it because you love me and you'll want to share it with me, but I just can't. It makes me cry just thinking about it.

Love,
Laurie

November 2

Dear Dad,

Mom says it's wrong of me to send you a letter that just says I'm miserable and unhappy and doesn't tell you why, so I guess I'll tell you, only if I start crying in the middle of this letter or screaming because now I'm mad too you'll have to understand.

Remember how excited I was about my birthday party? It was going to be the best party ever with all my best friends? It was HORRIBLE!!!!!!!!! It was even worse than that. Even Mom who's always saying things aren't as bad as I make them out to be said it was the worst birthday party she'd ever seen, and that for my twelfth birthday next year maybe I should leave the country.

I don't even know where to start, things were so bad. I guess everything began going wrong when Maria called to say she wouldn't be coming. It turned out her grandparents were in town and she never has a chance to see them, so her parents insisted she stay home even though she wanted to come to my party instead. I thought that would be okay, because frankly I never see Maria anymore, now that she's in whole different classes, but I wanted her here because she used to be one of my best friends and besides Shannon's been complaining lately because Maria never has any time for her, and they were best friends. Maria's new best friend is Gracie Schultz which drives Shannon double crazy because she and Maria always hated Gracie Schultz and now Maria's with her all the time and never does anything with Shannon.

Anyway Mom said if there were just five of us there'd be more for everybody, only she hid the leftover fudge because she decided she didn't want to share that. I've never seen anybody eat so much fudge so fast in my life, I think you'd better never send anymore to me or else Mom is going to end up looking like the Goodyear Blimp.

And then Mom and I went out to get my ears pierced, and I thought I could wear the beautiful pearl earrings you gave me right away, but the lady at the store popped different earrings into my ears (it pretty much didn't hurt) and said I had to wear those for a month until my ears healed. I love the way I look with earrings, and even Mom agreed they looked pretty.

Then we went home and straightened everything out. There already were streamers and balloons because Mom hung those up for me Thursday night after I went to bed so Friday morning when I woke up, the apartment looked birthdayish. But Mom had to do the dishes and hide the fudge so we kept busy.

And then everybody came, and you would have

thought things would be great except for Maria, only they were awful. First Jamie forgot to bring a costume, so we had to figure out what she could wear when we went trick-or-treating. Then Shannon got really upset because Maria wasn't coming. She said she bet Maria had lied about her grandparents because her grandparents live in Canada and they never come down for a visit so she was probably doing something with Gracie Schultz instead and I should never think of Maria as my friend again because she'd rather do something stupid with Gracie Schultz than go to my birthday party.

Maria really sounded like her grandparents had come and not like she was lying, and I told Shannon that, but she refused to believe me. She said Maria was nothing but a big two-faced liar and she wouldn't let any of her friends be friends with Maria too. I practically only invited Maria for Shannon's sake, and there Shannon was making me feel like a traitor because I had. Shannon sulked for the entire rest of the party. She fell asleep sulking and she woke up sulking the next day. She also wanted us to go to Maria's house and steal her Halloween costume so Jamie would have something to wear, which I thought was the most babyish thing I'd ever heard. And I wanted Darin and Jamie to like Shannon so I kept saying that Shannon was just upset and usually she was a lot of fun, and that made Shannon get mad at me and she even told me to shut up, which I thought was really rude since it was my birthday.

And you could see right off that Kris and Darin didn't like each other. They acted polite, but they hardly talked, so Darin and Jamie mostly stuck together and wouldn't talk to the rest of us. I brought out the magazines you sent and the two of them read one together, and they'd giggle at something and not tell us what they were laughing about. I think they were laughing at Shannon because once when I saw Shannon frowning I saw Darin make a big fake frown and Jamie really laughed then. And they kept talking about the great time we'd had together in summer camp, and they'd interrupt whatever was being said to ask me if I remembered when we'd done this or said that or if I'd heard from any of the other kids, which completely bored Kris.

I guess we went trick-or-treating like we were supposed to, and Jamie wore her jeans and an old T-shirt of Mom's that said Make Love Not War and Mom made a headband for her and said Jamie would just have to go as a hippie. Kris had this beautiful costume on which her mother had made for her. She was a circus star and it had a cape and bangles and she looked wonderful, but Darin said it looked kind of babyish to her and she thought Jamie's costume was perfect. Maybe she was trying to make Jamie feel better, but I don't think so. And Darin's costume was exactly the same as mine; we both bought the same witch outfit at the five-and-ten. Darin and I always did that at camp, thought the same things, and bought the same stuff, but I could see Kris was mad because her mother made such a beautiful costume but none of us made a fuss about it because we were so busy trying to figure out what Jamie could wear and Darin and I thought it was so amazing that we had the exact same costumes. Meanwhile Shannon said she was

41

too upset to go trick-or-treating and she was just going to stay in the apartment with Mom because she didn't want to risk seeing Maria trick-or-treating with Gracie Schultz which was basically impossible because Maria and Gracie both live blocks and blocks away and would never come here to trick-or-treat. Anyway Mom said it was okay if Shannon stayed with her even though she thought Shannon would have a better time going with the rest of us.

We went to a few apartments and got a bunch of stuff, but then Jamie said she'd better stop because her mother never lets her eat sugar (she ate candy all the time at camp, and cookies and cake and it never bothered her once), and she'd promised her mother she wouldn't eat too much. She said when she eats too much sugar she gets real hyper and screams all the time and then she screamed to show us and half the doors opened to see what was going on and Kris was so embarrassed and she said that was such a baby thing to do, screaming like that and Jamie said, "It takes one to know one," and then she and Darin started giggling again. So we went back home and I didn't get nearly as much stuff as I'd wanted and it wasn't like there was that much fudge left and even if there was Mom wasn't going to let me near it. I really love Mom but it turns out she's totally untrustworthy around fudge.

When we got back, Mom was on the phone and Shannon was watching TV, so Mom hung up fast and called to order us our pizza, only it turned out none of us wanted the same things on it, so it took forever to decide and when we finally did nobody was happy. I like mushrooms and onions, and Jamie hates mushrooms and Darin hates onions and Shannon hates pepperoni which Kris suggested and Kris hates anchovies which Darin suggested and Mom said it would be easier to negotiate an arms treaty than it was to figure out what kind of pizza we wanted. We ended up getting plain so we were all bored.

And while we were waiting for the pizza none of us knew what to do so Jamie and Darin started giggling again and Darin made Jamie scream for real so she'd know what Jamie sounded like when she truly got hyper and Shannon said all the screaming was giving her a headache and then the pizza came only they delivered a regular instead of an extra large so there wasn't enough for us. Mom didn't have any, and even so there wasn't enough, and Kris said if we were going to get a regular-sized pizza then we could have gotten two of them so one could have been half mushroom and half onion and the other could have been half pepperoni and half anchovies and then everybody would have been happy and Darin said it was a shame Kris didn't think to suggest that in the first place and she guessed that was how it was with gifted and talented people, they could figure out what to do but not in time to do it.

So then Kris got mad and asked what Darin meant by that, and Darin said some people thought they were really special, but at least she knew her lefts and rights. And Kris said to me, "You told her that?" and that got Jamie laughing again and I thought Kris was going to scream.

So Mom stepped in and said, "I thought this was supposed to be a birthday party with cake and ghost stories," and Jamie said how she couldn't have any cake so why didn't we have the ghost stories instead. And Mom said there was a special treat, that you'd sent us that videotape and she'd left it in the VCR so when we were ready for it, it would be right there. We all walked over to the TV, and the VCR was running, and Shannon said, "Oh yeah, when you all came in, I started recording the show I was watching," and we turned the VCR off fast, and rewound the tape, and half of your beautiful tape was recorded over. That was the worst thing that happened in that whole horrible day, and Shannon didn't even apologize. She just said people who leave tapes in machines shouldn't be surprised when other people recorded on them.

Mom said it would be okay, you could make me another tape, but Daddy, I loved that tape so much, and I was going to watch it every single day, just so I could see you and hear your voice, and now it's gone, and so are all my friendships. We kept on with the sleepover because it was easier than sending everybody back home, and we ate the birthday cake (Jamie managed to eat two and half pieces) and when I blew out the candles I wished that everybody would just go away, but they didn't until the next morning.

I guess breakfast would have been okay if we'd all been speaking to each other, but since nobody liked anybody at that point, none of us were upset when everybody went home. I spent the rest of Sunday crying. Mom finished the fudge. She said she didn't want me to learn to turn to sweets when my life was going bad, but sometimes chocolate really was the answer. She ate twice as much as I did, but I was too upset to eat.

I don't even have Jimmy as a friend anymore. He told me in school today that he was wrong, some queers do like girls as friends, and since he doesn't want to be a queer, we can't be friends anymore.

Mom says this will all pass and someday I'll look back on all of it and cry a little less hard, but I don't see how I can ever be happy again.

Love,
Laurie

November 7

Dear Dad,

I hate school and I hate not having friends and I hate being eleven. The only good thing that happened all week was Darin sent me a note apologizing for the way she behaved. I wish Kris had manners like that since she's the one I go to school with who's supposed to be my best friend, but she's acted like it was all my fault everything was so awful because I told Darin she couldn't tell her lefts from her rights. Well, she can't. I don't understand how anybody that stupid could be in the gifted and talented program when I'm not.

Kris was awful to me all week just because I told the truth. On Thursday they announced a special pen pal program and said we could sign up for pen pals if we wanted. So at lunch I told Kris I wanted to, but since I wrote to you every week, I wasn't sure I'd have time to write to a pen pal too. And Kris said, "Us gifted and talented people can write letters to more than one person," and signed up for two pen pals that afternoon. So I signed up for one, too, just to show her. She thinks she's the most gifted and talented person in the world, but I agree with Darin. People who can't tell their lefts from their rights shouldn't think they're as gifted and talented as other people who can even if they're not in some stupid program.

Love,
Laurie

P.S. Before I put this letter in the envelope Mom asked me what I'd written you. Actually she said, "I hope you didn't write your father a letter all about how sorry you're feeling for yourself, because frankly, it's getting to be a little boring." So I said I didn't write anything about how sorry I felt for myself, just about how Kris didn't deserve to be in the gifted and talented program and I did. So Mom sighed (she's really been acting sorry for herself since she's finished all the fudge) and said if it's that important to me to be in the gifted and talented program, why didn't I talk to the teacher in charge and see if I could convince her to put me in.

Sometimes I think Mom is the smartest woman in the universe. It never occurred to me that I could just ask. I'm going to on Monday. And I'm sure I'll be able to convince them and then I'll be in the program too.

What would be best is if they have to kick Kris

out to make room for me, but second best would be seeing her face when I'm in there with her. I bet once I get in, I'll be a hundred times more gifted and talented than she is.

P.P.S. I told Mom about how I wrote how smart she is and how much more gifted and talented I was going to be than Kris once I got in, and Mom said she didn't know why I was so mad at Kris. She said, "All your friends behaved like monsters, but Kris was the least awful one in my opinion." Nowadays Mom shudders if I even mention Jamie's name to her. I can't explain why I'm so mad at Kris, but if she'd only liked Darin everything would have been okay, and it's like she wasn't willing to even try and it was my birthday and I am supposed to be her best friend and now I guess she figures she's too gifted and talented for the likes of me. I'll show her.

November 14

Dear Dad,

I really thought I'd be writing to you on Monday to tell you all about how I'm in the gifted and talented program now, only I didn't even know until Thursday that I wasn't going to be and that's just the way my entire life has been lately, and Mom says November isn't even half over with and if it isn't May next week she's going to quit teaching and run away to Tahiti and not take me with her, thank you very much.

I don't see what she's so mad about when it was her idea that I ask the teacher in charge of the gifted and talented program to put me in. Mom gets mad sometimes when she really shouldn't. I told her that and she said, "Yes, absolutely, there's a contract mothers sign when they get their babies swearing that they'll turn into irrational maniacs just to drive their poor innocent children crazy and you'll be much better off when I'm in Tahiti all by myself." I made her repeat that so I could memorize it and write it to you and that way I know that's exactly what she said. November had better turn into May real fast.

Anyway, on Monday I went to the office and said I wanted to talk to the teacher in charge of the gifted and talented program, and they looked at me like nobody had ever asked them for that name before and who was I and what right did I have to ask them anything? I guess they thought they could scare me away, but they couldn't. I simply said, "I need to speak to the teacher in charge of the gifted and talented program," like I was a grown-up, and they hemmed and hawed and then they found the name and gave it to me. Mrs. Coleman, room 227. This was after school on Monday, because I'd been real mature, and hadn't rushed in there to get her name, but waited until school was over. Also, I'd gotten a late start that morning, and I didn't really have time before school to ask.

So I went up to room 227 and Mrs. Coleman was there, I guessed, because I'd never met Mrs. Coleman, so I said, "Hello, I want to find out why I'm not in the gifted and talented program," and Mrs. Coleman said, "I don't know what you're talking about," and I said, "I deserve to be in the gifted and talented program at least as much as Kris Chandler," without mentioning about how Kris can't tell her lefts from her rights, and Mrs. Coleman said, "I'm sorry, but I'm just a substitute; Mrs. Coleman is out sick today, she should be back tomorrow."

Why couldn't she have told me that in the first place instead of waiting for me to make a total fool of myself? I really hate teachers sometimes, and grown-ups. Anyway, I apologized and waited until Tuesday, and then after school, I went back to room 227, only the substitute was still there. And then Wednesday, there wasn't any school, and Mom and I went shopping for stuff for me to take to Missouri and Florida and we went to the movies and had a nice day. Mom says I have to tell you when we have nice days, or else you'll think all she ever does for me is eat my fudge and make my life miserable.

So then Thursday afternoon came, and it had been this terrible week, because all I'd been thinking about all week long was how I was going to ask Mrs. Coleman to put me in the gifted and talented program and she was out sick and I couldn't tell Kris what I was doing because then it wouldn't be a surprise. Kris thinks we're friends again, and I decided we would be once I was in the gifted and talented program same as her. I decided I didn't want them to kick her out, I wanted her there so she could see how much more gifted and talented I was and then she'd really appreciate me. We got back two tests this week, and I got higher grades than she did in both of them, but she said she wasn't feeling well the day we took those tests, that she hadn't felt well all last week and she thought it was because of the pizza at my party, as though the rest of us hadn't eaten that exact same pizza and been perfectly fine. I told Mom that, and Mom said the pizza was the least of what went wrong at my party.

When the bell rang Thursday afternoon, Kris asked me if I wanted to go to her house and we could do our homework together, and study for a big French test we had on Friday, but I said no, only I didn't tell her why. I just went back to room 227, and this time there was a woman there who wasn't the same one who'd been there Monday and Tuesday, but just to be on the safe side I asked her if she was Mrs. Coleman, and she said she was.

So I said, "My name is Laurie Levine and I'm in sixth grade and I want to be in the gifted and talented program too," which was probably a better way of doing it than saying I deserved to be more than Kris. Monday evening Mom and I talked about what I should say to Mrs. Coleman and Mom said I shouldn't sound too demanding or whiny, and I figured since Mom's a teacher, she should know.

So Mrs. Coleman told me to sit down, which I did, and she sat down on the edge of her desk and asked me why I wanted to be in the gifted and talented program. The funny thing was, I didn't have an answer. If she'd asked me why I deserved to be, then I would have had a lot to tell her, including Kris's lefts and rights. But it was hard to say why I wanted to be, so I just said, "One of my friends is in it and it sounds like fun."

"We try to make the gifted and talented program entertaining," Mrs. Coleman said, "But it's more than that. It's a lot of work too."

So I said I knew that, and I wasn't afraid of work and that I had very good grades, some of them were even better than the grades of at least one person in the gifted and talented program, but I didn't say whose just in case it really was the pizza that made Kris do worse than me on those tests.

Mrs. Coleman said she was sure I was very smart, but they'd had to leave a lot of kids out of the program who were also very smart, because there wasn't room for too many kids, and they found that around sixty was the best number and that was for the entire school. She said it was a real shame that everybody couldn't be in the gifted and talented program, but then again, everybody wasn't gifted and talented, at least not at Baker, and she was sure my parents would be happy to do lots of culturally enriching stuff with me that would be just as good as the gifted and talented program. I guess I'd mentioned that Mom taught at the high school.

So I tried to think about all the culturally enriching stuff Mom and I did together, only the movie we'd seen on Wednesday was *Bubble Bath* rated PG-13, and the only culturally enriching stuff in it were its nude scenes, which Mom made me cover my eyes for anyway. (I peeked.) So I said Mom didn't have time to be culturally enriching because it was hard work teaching high school history and you weren't around to do culturally enriching stuff with because you were in Missouri and it wasn't fair that I was being deprived of all this culturally enriching stuff because I wasn't in the gifted and talented program when I deserved to be.

You know that look Mom gets when I say something isn't fair after she's already told me no? Mrs. Coleman must be a mother too, because she looked the exact same way. I think the only thing that kept her from saying, "Life isn't fair," was that I'm not her daughter. Instead she said, "I'm sorry, but we've already selected the students for the gifted and talented program. Better luck next year." So I said, "Please, I promise I'll be extremely gifted and talented," and she said, "I already said no twice; how many more times do you have to hear it?" so I left. And Kris was still in the schoolyard when I got there, and she said, "I figured I'd wait for you in case you changed your mind. Where were you?" and I couldn't tell her, so I just walked home without saying a word to her. So in school yesterday, she wouldn't talk to me either, which I think was really babyish of her but what do you expect from someone like that? At least Darin wrote to say she was sorry.

I really hate sixth grade.

Anyway, I kind of had this idea, which I haven't told Mom yet, and maybe you won't like it either, but if when I visit you at Thanksgiving, if I really love Missouri, could I maybe stay with you for the rest of the year? You said your apartment has an extra bedroom just for me and if I can live with Mom and eat pizza and Chinese take-out, then I can live with you and eat pizza and Chinese take-out too. And I bet the kids in Missouri are much nicer than the ones here, so I could make wonderful new friends, and I'm really much neater than I used to be when you and Mom were married. I make my bed and hang up my coat without being asked. I know Mom loves me, and I guess she'd miss me, but frankly, I think she'd like a vacation from me for a few months. What do you think?

> Love,
> Laurie

P.S. Don't tell Mom about me living with you in case I hate Missouri.
P.P.S. I miss you all the time.

November 19

Dear Dad,

Usually I write to you on weekends, but I'm going to be seeing you in a week, and I figured if I wrote you on Saturday, my letter and I would come practically the same time so I'm writing to you today instead. I hope you don't mind.

Kris did better than me on our French test and our math test, so maybe it really was the pizza that made her do so badly the week before. We're talking again, which is more than I'm doing with Shannon or Jimmy. Darin called me Sunday. We hadn't spoken since my birthday party, and it was kind of weird talking with her at first, but then I told her about Mrs. Coleman, and she agreed with me that is wasn't fair that I wasn't in the program. She said Mrs. Coleman should let anybody in who wanted to be culturally enriched and I think so too.

I got my pen pal. Her name is Victoria Rosamond James (isn't that the prettiest name you ever heard?)

and she lives in Keighly, England. I looked Keighly up in our atlas, and it seems to be in the middle of England somewhere. Mom said in Yorkshire. She says that's Brontë country, but I don't know what she means, and I never got around to asking. I guess if I had she could have culturally enriched me but there was something on TV I wanted to watch instead. Anyway, I wrote to Victoria Rosamond James and told her all about myself and about you and Mom and Kris and Darin and Ross Perlman and the gifted and talented program, and now I guess she'll write back to me, and tell me all about herself. Do you think they have gifted and talented programs in England? Mom says that for the sake of all the mothers and fathers of England, she hopes not.

Mom also says she'll call you Monday night to confirm all the arrangements and that she hopes I'll have a wonderful time in Missouri and take lots of good pictures for my class project. She's been teaching me how to use her camera, and she says if I really like taking pictures then she'll get me a camera of my own for Chanukah and I'll be able to take it to Florida during winter vacation. She said for me to tell you all that in case you were thinking of buying me a camera too.

And she also says that even though it won't exactly be a full month since I got my ears pierced, she thinks it'll be okay if I wear the pearl earrings you gave me when I visit you so you can see how beautiful my pierced ears are. She also says that under no circumstances are you to give me any fudge to take home. Mom's been very sensitive about that fudge ever since she weighed herself right after my birthday.

Mom got me this really pretty dress for when we go out to dinner on Thanksgiving and a new pair of jeans and two new shirts. I've grown two inches since I got back from summer camp, and she says you won't recognize me, so I guess I'll have to recognize you at the airport instead!

I CAN'T WAIT! ! !

Love,
Laurie

November 25

Dear Dad,

I hate you and I never want to speak to you again or write you any more letters and I wish you weren't my father.

Laura Diane Levine

November 26

Dear Dad,

Mom says it's Thanksgiving and I have a lot to be grateful for, and I should write to you and tell

you that and tell you I love you and that I'm sorry
only I'm not sorry and I don't love you and I have
nothing to be grateful for and sometimes I hate
Mom too because she doesn't understand.

You knew how much I was looking forward to
seeing you. You knew it was the most important
thing in the world to me. But you cancelled out
anyway.

Mom says it wasn't your fault, that Gramps got
sick and had to go into the hospital and that Nana
needed you there to help her with everything, but
I don't see why I couldn't have gone down to Florida
and been with all of you instead of stuck here the
way I always am. Mom says Gramps isn't going to
die and I should be grateful for that, but I don't see
why he had to get sick the day before I was supposed
to go to Missouri or why you had to stay in Florida
once you knew he wasn't going to die after all.

Mom says I should be grown-up and understand-
ing, that you must have been scared and upset about
Gramps, the way Nana was when she called you,
but I don't care what you felt. You don't care what
I feel. I know you don't love me. You may think
that's a secret, but I figured it out. I bet Mom knows,
too, but she's pretending not to because she doesn't
like to say mean things about you. In all her divorce
books that I read, it says you should never say bad
things about your child's father, and that's why she
doesn't tell me the truth, that you don't love me,
but it doesn't matter because I know anyway.

Sure you said you love me, that you'd always love
me, that the divorce didn't have anything to do with
me or the way you love me, but if you really loved

me, you and Mom would never have gotten a divorce.

And even if you had, you wouldn't have moved a thousand miles away from me, two cars and two plane rides, just for some stupid job. When you first got that job, Mom said it was a job you'd dreamed of having for years and years and she was thrilled for you, and I should be too, but I hated it for taking you away and I hated you for going. I didn't say so because Mom said that wouldn't be fair, that you shouldn't think I'd stop loving you just because you were far away, anymore than you'd stop loving me. She said I should write you letters so you could see what my life was like, and you'd write back and call me and we'd have time to visit during vacations. And I did what she told me. I only cried a little when we went out for supper right before you moved, and I wrote you those stupid letters every single week and I kept on loving you.

Only now you've shown everybody that you don't love me, and I won't pretend anymore, and I refuse to write letters to you or talk to you on the phone or see you ever. I hope Mom falls in love and gets married again and I have a brand-new father.

I hate you forever.

> Your former daughter,
> Laurie

Dear Dad,

Yesterday I wrote you a terrible letter and it said I hated you and you didn't love me, and I was mad, I mailed it right off, but I hardly slept at all last night, thinking about you reading the letter, and I wanted to call you today, to tell you not to open it, but Mom says you're still in Florida and we shouldn't bother you when Gramps is still sick. So if you find both letters at the same time, when you get home, read this one, and don't read the other. Just tear it up because otherwise you really might hate me for writing all those mean things.

I wrote the letter because it made me really mad that you cancelled my visit. I know it wasn't your fault that Gramps got sick, but it made me feel like you didn't love me, because if you did, then you wouldn't let so much time go by without seeing me, and then when I was finally going to come out, you said no. I don't think I've ever been so angry in my life, except maybe when you moved out. It hurts like that when I don't see you.

I'm going to put Open This Letter First on the envelope so you'll know to open it. I really do love you. I just hate not seeing you. Mom said if I didn't love you, I wouldn't mind not seeing you at all, and after I thought about it, I realized she was right.

I hope Gramps is feeling better. I hope I can see you again sometime soon.

Love,
Laurie

November 30

Dear Dad,

Mom's made all the reservations, and I'll be arriving in Columbus at five-thirteen Friday afternoon. I don't believe you and Mom both decided I could miss school on Friday and Monday just so I could have some time alone with you!

I loved talking with you on Sunday. Thank you for not opening that stupid letter I sent. I will never ever tell you I hate you. All I want is to see you and I will in four days! ! !

        Love,
        Laurie

December 10

Dear Dad,

I bet that was the best visit any daughter ever had with her father, don't you? My favorite part was Saturday when we went for that walk and just talked about school and your new job and stuff. I also loved it when you showed me your office and introduced me to all the people you work with. And going to the football game at your school was great, even if your team lost. I bet after you've been assistant superintendent of schools longer, you'll have a champion football team.

It's funny how before Thanksgiving I really hated school and all my friends and life, and now I think everything's terrific. I've even forgiven Shannon for taping over the videotape of you. She and Kris came over for supper yesterday and I told them all about Missouri and my visit with you. And Mom says I can call Darin tomorrow and tell her too. So that only leaves Jamie and Maria and Jimmy of my ex-friends. Maria has gotten real dumb since she started hanging out with Gracie Schultz, so I don't care about her anymore, and once you've spent an evening listening to Jamie scream you don't want to spend any more time with her. So that really only leaves Jimmy, and I think he's ready to be friends again too.

And I got my first letter from Victoria Rosamond James. She signed the letter just Victoria, but I love her whole name so much that's what I always think of her as. Kris got two pen pals, but one is named Edith Smythe and the other is named Marjorie Firth, so I figured Victoria Rosamond James is worth at least two Ediths and Marjories. Anyway, Victoria Rosamond James says Keighly is right next door to Haworth, which is where the Brontës used to live, and she's eleven years old, same as me, and she rides horses and draws and her favorite actor is Ross Perlman too! She says they get to see lots of American TV shows in England, and half the girls in her class have a crush on him. But you can tell she's English, because she spells some words funny (she said Ross Perlman was her "favourite" and Mom had to tell me that's how they spell it there) and she says she likes tea and biscuits, and Mom had to explain that biscuits are really just boring cookies. I can see how having a pen pal is going to be a very culturally enriching experience.

Speaking of being culturally enriched, Mom says we haven't been doing enough of that lately. She says we've been watching too much TV (I think she got upset when she realized I didn't know who the Brontës are. Now I know. They lived in the nineteenth century and were sisters and wrote novels, all of which seem to be Mom's number one favorite. Or favourite!). So this weekend, we're going to go to the city and spend the afternoon at a museum. Mom hasn't decided which one yet.

Also, even though I missed two days at school, I don't seem to have missed anything. I had a French test today, and I think I got everything right. And even math seems less horrible than it used to be.

Mom says nobody in their right minds likes December except during the holidays, but I like it right now.

You know what I like best about the Brontës? Those dots over their ë. From now on, I'm dotting Laurie.

Love,
Laurië

December 13

Dear Dad,

I still love December, but I have a cold. Mom made me stay home from school yesterday, because I had a fever. Not a real high one, so she went to work, but enough to keep me home. Also I've been blowing my nose all day (I've been through two boxes of tissues already), and I sneezed twelve times in an hour and a half and my throat hurts too.

Mom made me chicken soup, and bought three different flavors of ice cream, and rented *The Wizard of Oz* and *Little Women* for me to watch. She says we won't be going to the museum this weekend though, because I should get really well before running around. She also says I'd better be one hundred percent healthy before vacation, so I can have a wonderful time in Florida. She says Nana says Gramps is healthy enough for me to visit and that he'd be heartbroken if I didn't come.

Oops. I sneezed three more times, once on this letter. I hope you don't catch the cold from me.

> Love,
> Laurie

December 15

Dear Dad,

We go on vacation next Wednesday, and it seems like our teachers want to work us to death before we leave. Then they want to work us to death while we're away too. So my science project on Neptune is due Friday, and my project on Missouri is due the day I get back. Also I have a book report due on Thursday, and a math test on Friday and I have to write a two-page composition in French for next Tuesday, and I don't know even a page's worth of French words. We can write about anything we want, so I'm going to write about how I'm going to Florida to visit you and Gramps and Nana. I know the French words for father and grandfather and grandmother and sick and I don't have to know the French words for Florida and Missouri, so I figure I'm almost halfway there.

Neptune turns out to be a very boring planet. I probably should have picked Mercury which is small and hot and moves around real fast. Or Venus which is beautiful and full of gaseous clouds. Or Jupiter which is big or Pluto which is small. Or Saturn which has rings, or Mars, which maybe has life, or even Uranus which sounds like a dirty word. Oh well. Next solar system, I'll know better.

I wrote a long letter to Victoria Rosamond James. I told her I'd send her pictures from Florida. She wrote in her letter that she knows about Florida because a friend of hers once went to Disney World. Isn't that funny? I didn't know people in England had ever heard of Disney World. She says her friend brought her back Mickey Mouse ears as a souvenir. Mom says I don't have to bring her back anything from Florida, especially anything edible. She's been on a diet for the past few days and she even turns the TV off when there's a food commercial. She says she wants to lose weight before New Year's, so she won't have to make any resolutions except to get her paperwork done faster.

Kris is going to Indiana for Christmas, and Shannon's staying home with her family. Darin and her family are going to Los Angeles for the vacation. Her aunt and uncle live there. She says they'll go to Disneyland. I said if you took me to Disney World, I'd buy her Mickey Mouse ears, and she should buy me Mickey Mouse ears from Disneyland and then we wouldn't have to worry if we'd like what we got each other. Darin said that was an extremely gifted and talented gift.

I can't wait until next week. Can you?

Love,
Laurie

January 3

Dear Dad,

Mom asked me if I'd thought about New Year's resolutions while I was in Florida, and I told her I wanted to see more of you and to work harder at school and not to be jealous of other people. Mom said those were the three best resolutions she'd ever heard, except for her mother's when Gran resolved to quit smoking and she actually did. I never even knew Gran smoked so she must have resolved that a long time ago.

Anyway Mom said my resolution to see more of you was a very smart one, and she hoped we could, but I should realize that you were very busy, and I was very busy too, so we might not be able to see each other as much as we might like but that we'd have to have a long talk about what I was going to do this summer.

So I said I thought I'd go back to summer camp, and Mom said I could if I wanted, but maybe I'd prefer to spend just half the summer there, and half with you, and I said that was the most wonderful idea I ever heard of and that she was very very smart. So Mom said, "Yes, absolutely, I am the smartest mother in the world, but actually it was your father's idea, so I guess he's the smartest father in the world too." Then she said since I had such a smart mother and such a smart father, I must be a pretty smart daughter, and we hugged then, and kissed, and agreed it was very nice to be so smart and wonderful.

I got a letter yesterday from Victoria Rosamond James, who thanked me for all the postcards I sent her from Disney World. Her letters are nearly as long as mine are, only I have to write to her and to you, and she just has to write to me. Of course now she signs her letters to me Victoria Rosamond James because that's how I address her, and that adds to the time it takes to write. Kris has only gotten one letter from Edith Smythe, but she says Marjorie What's-her-name writes all the time. That's what she calls her, Marjorie What's-her-name. She doesn't like her at all. Kris had a real good time in Indiana, even though she said it was freezing and it snowed nearly every day so they hardly got any shopping done. And Darin had a great time in Los Angeles, where it didn't snow at all. And Shannon had a good time at home.

School starts tomorrow. I think my project on

Missouri is terrific, because of all the help you gave me, and since I'm now officially the smartest daughter in the world, I think I should do pretty well.
                    Love,
                    Laurie

P.S. Mom says if you aren't jealous of other people like the resolution I made, you also don't lord it over people if you have something better than they do. But I'm still glad I got Victoria Rosamond James as a pen pal, and Kris got stuck with Edith and Marjorie.

                                        January 9

Dear Dad,
    It snowed seven inches Thursday night. Mom and I watched the snow fall instead of TV and she told me stories from when she was a kid. She told me about the time she fell out of the tree and nearly broke her leg only she didn't want her parents to know she'd been in the tree because they had forbidden her to climb it, so she kept trying not to limp whenever she walked near them. And then she told me she never wanted me climbing trees or disobeying her, but then she made us both hot chocolate and told me about how she used to want to be a movie star and change her name to Gloria Adair because she thought that was such a beautiful name.

We stayed up really late, because we were both so sure there'd be no school the next day and we were right. We would have slept late, except Kris's mother called us up in the morning and said Kris had a snow day but she and Kris's father didn't, and would Mom mind if she dropped Kris off to spend the day with us stay-at-homes. Mom said it was fine with her, and I got to spend the day playing with Kris. Mom insisted we do some homework, since we don't have school on Monday because it's Martin Luther King's birthday and she felt it was wrong if we all waited until last thing Monday night to do our work. She did her paperwork too, while Kris and I worked.

But once we were finished, Mom said what this apartment complex really needed was a snowman, so we all went outside and built one. When we started, it was just the three of us, and frankly I was a little embarrassed, in case Kris thought making a snow man was a baby thing to do, but Kris really enjoyed making it, and after a while other people joined us, and soon there were nearly twenty of us, mostly kids, but some grown-ups, out there making snowmen. We ended up with quite an army of them. We sang too. Thank goodness that wasn't Mom's idea, but one of the little kids started singing "Jingle Bells," so we all joined in, and then we sang other songs while we built our snowmen. One woman kept trying to make a snowwoman, but her breasts kept falling off, so she ended up being a snowman too. The woman said that symbolized the injustice of the relationships between men and women in this world, and Mom said that while that was true, Kris and I were too young to hear it, so she pretended to cover our ears. Kris said her father said it was men who had it the roughest, and Mom and the woman both laughed.

That reminds me. I never told you, but after I got back from Florida, I told Mom that you told Nana you were dating again, and she said that was nice, but that night, I could hear her crying. Mom cries sometimes when we watch a sad movie, but I got up and checked, and there were no lights on in her room, so I think she was crying because of what I told her. I didn't tell her I'd heard her cry, and maybe I shouldn't tell you, but Mom says I should always be honest to you in my letters, although that doesn't mean I have a license to complain all the time.

Anyway, after Kris left, Mom decided that since we had all this extra time this weekend, we should spend it spring-cleaning, so when it was spring, we wouldn't have to spring-clean and could do nice stuff instead. So all weekend long we've been cleaning and scrubbing. Mom cleaned the oven, and you know how much she hates doing that, and she climbed up the stepladder, and removed all the light fixtures and cleaned them, and I dusted all the books (which took forever!), and Mom is out there cleaning this very minute, but I told her I had to write you a letter, because she told me I had to way back last spring, and I always do just what she wants. She laughed, and told me not to make it too long a letter because we still had a lot of cleaning left to go. Mom gets this crazed look in her eyes when she's cleaning. I'm glad she doesn't mind that usually we're sloppy.

I'd better not take any chances. I think I'll get back to cleaning before Mom thinks I've been gone too long, and starts mistaking me for Cinderella.

Love,
Laurie

January 17

Dear Dad,

You know how I resolved never to be jealous of my friends again? Well, I really have been a lot less jealous, although it made me mad that Kris got a 97 on her report on comets, and I only got a 90 on Neptune, which was a much harder topic because Neptune turned out to be so boring. But even Mom says I'm better than I used to be and she's proud of me for trying.

Well I'm jealous again, and it's not my fault. I'd say it was Kris's but I guess it wasn't hers either. I don't know whose fault it was but it makes me mad I feel this way.

Here's what happened. On Tuesday I went back to school with all my schoolwork done, and the apartment as clean as it's ever been and practically before I got through the door, Kris was standing there telling me that Kelly Dale had left Baker because her parents finally got their divorce and her mother had said as soon as the divorce was final she was getting out of this town and never wanted to see anybody here ever again. Kris and Kelly were pretty good friends, so that's how Kris knew all that. I never much liked Kelly so I didn't care if she moved or not and I told Kris that, but Kris said, "Put your gifted and talented brain to work and you'll realize that Kelly was in the gifted and talented program, which means there's an opening, so why don't you ask Mrs. Coleman if you can join now?"

Actually, now that I think about it, it was really pretty nice of Kris to think of that, when all I'd done all year long was complain because she was in the gifted and talented program and I wasn't. And Mrs. Coleman had said that the reason I couldn't be in the gifted and talented program was because they only liked to have sixty kids in it, and now they had fifty-nine. And Kelly was in sixth grade, same as me, so it was a sixth-grade opening. At lunch Kris told me again I should talk to Mrs. Coleman. She said Mrs. Coleman was really very nice once you got to know her, and I'd love being in the gifted and talented program, and I was at least as smart as half the kids in it, if not more and I could tell Mrs. Coleman she said so.

So after school that day, I went to Mrs. Coleman's room and there she was. I have to admit, it scared me to talk to her again, but I remembered what Kris told me and I walked in. She didn't remember who I was, until I said I wanted to talk to her about the new opening in the gifted and talented program.

"Oh, that's right," she said. "It's you."

I didn't know how to answer that, because of course it was me, you didn't have to be gifted and talented to know that. So I just nodded.

Mrs. Coleman stared at me, and I got the feeling she wished I wasn't there, but I was. I kind of wished I wasn't there too, but it was too late, and besides, I never disappear when I want to. Have you ever noticed that? The less you want to be someplace, the harder it is for you to be someplace else. Sometimes when I'm at the dentist's I think I've been there since the moment I was born it feels like so long. I almost mentioned that to Mrs. Coleman only there didn't seem much point.

Instead I said that I knew Kelly Dale was leaving because her parents were finally divorced, and she was definitely never coming back because her mother hated it here, so Kelly's place in the gifted and talented program was open forever, and that meant there were only fifty-nine people in the program so could I be number sixty because if anything I was even more gifted and talented than I had been in November.

"Oh?" She said. "How?"

I really felt like I was in the dentist's chair then, but I said, "I've grown up a lot in the past couple of months because my grandfather got sick so I couldn't spend Thanksgiving with my father and I got really mad and I learned that you don't care if you don't see someone unless you really love them and I don't get jealous as much as I used to and I have a pen pal named Victoria Rosamond James and I've been to Disney World and learned that Neptune is a truly boring planet."

Mrs. Coleman looked like she couldn't decide whether she wanted to laugh or cry. "My," she said.

"That certainly is a lot of growth in the gifted and talented department."

So I agreed with her. "I used to be just gifted and talented," I said. "Now I'm very gifted and talented."

Mrs. Coleman nodded, and I thought that meant she was going to put me in the program. But instead she said, "My experience with gifted and talented people is they don't talk all that much about themselves, because they're so interested in everything that's going on around them."

I knew then she was definitely talking about me. "Like me right now!" I said. "The way I've been talking about Kelly Dale. I guess that really proves how gifted and talented I've become since the last time we talked."

"No, Laurie," Mrs. Coleman said. "Your name is Laurie, isn't it?"

I don't get discouraged easily, Dad, but if she still wasn't sure what my name was, I figured I hadn't done that great a job convincing her to put me in the stupid program. And it must be a stupid program if she wouldn't let me in. I'd proven to her over and over again just how gifted and talented I was, and she still could hardly remember my name. Of course one of the times I'd convinced her, I'd actually convinced the substitute by mistake, but I bet the substitute told her about me, so that time should count too. I wanted to cry when she asked me if my name was Laurie. I also wanted to complain to the principal that the teacher in charge of the gifted and talented program couldn't be all that gifted and talented herself if she couldn't even remember my name. Only instead of crying or complaining, I just said, "One day I'll prove to you how gifted and talented I really am and then you'll ask me to be in your program." That's truly what I said. What I thought was they'd beg me to be in their stupid program, but I didn't say beg and I didn't say stupid. I think I scowled though, and then I thanked her and left her stupid room.

Part of me feels Kris should drop out of the program since they won't take me in, but I know that's selfish, so I haven't asked her. Besides, she should think of it herself. I would do the same for her. I dropped out of Brownies, after all, when she had to switch times on her piano lessons and couldn't go anymore. Of course, I didn't like being a Brownie, but that's beside the point. I would have stayed with it if she had, but as soon as she couldn't, I dropped out.

I'm a gifted and talented friend too, and someday I'll invent a program for us unrecognized gifted and talented people, and I'll sell it to all the schools and make lots and lots of money and be world famous, and probably then Mrs. Coleman will beg me to be in her stupid program, only I'll say no and that'll serve her right.

Love,
Laurie

P.S. Mom asked me once what kind of stuff I write you, and I told her, and she said, "Don't you ever tell him the good stuff? It sounds like all you do is complain." I told her that you didn't mind, that you loved me because you were my father, and you were always on my side, especially when I was right like I am this time. Mom laughed then. I know Mom loves me a lot, but sometimes she'd love me even more if I lived two plane rides and two car rides away. I know there are times I'd love her more if she did.

January 21

Dear Dad,
Mom is going out on a date Saturday night. I just thought you ought to know.

Love,
Laurie

January 24

Dear Dad,
Mom went out on a date last night. I wrote to you on Thursday, as soon as I knew, but I guess if you got my letter in time, you couldn't think what to do about it either.

She went out with Mr. Calegari. He's the new gym teacher at the high school. I heard Mom talking to her friend Sheila on the phone and Mom said it would be nice to go out with a man with a good body for a change, and then she giggled and Sheila must have said something very funny because she laughed even harder then.

Mr. Calegari's first name is Bruno and I think that's the ugliest name I ever heard, Bruno Calegari. It sounds like a wrestler, and I told him so, and he laughed and said he used to wrestle in high school and college, and he always felt his name gave him a real advantage, especially when he wrestled against guys with names like Jack Feldman and Percy Entwhistle, and Mom laughed and said, "You never really wrestled anybody named Percy Ent-whistle," and Mr. Calegari said, "Yes I did, and he was real tough. You'd be tough too if your name was Percy Entwhistle," and Mom laughed nearly as hard as she had when she was talking with Sheila. I practically puked.

The whole day was awful. Mom kept changing her mind about what to wear and she kept asking my opinion, like I cared. Remember that time you and she went to that party, and she tried on five different dresses? It was like that only worse. She even ran out in the middle of the afternoon to buy a new dress, and she came back with three, only she decided she'd return them all Monday after school. So finally she put on the dress she'd tried on first (big surprise), and then she took it off to shower again, and she called Sheila for "encour-agement" and then she got dressed for the eigh-teenth time and asked me for the hundred-twenty-third time how she looked and I said fine, even though I thought the dress made her look fat.

I was supposed to spend the night at Kris's only Kris caught a cold and wasn't in school yesterday, so Mom found a babysitter for me, and I haven't had a babysitter in years because Mom doesn't go out anymore, and when she does, she takes me with her. I offered to go with her and Mr. Calegari, and that made her giggle some more. Actually it was a short giggle and a fast "no." She finally got the friend of one of her students to babysit, some dumb girl named Judy who insisted on watching what she wanted to watch on TV and ate practically all the cookies Mom bought on Friday. I stayed in my room and did my homework, I was so disgusted.

Judy thought Mr. Calegari was cute. She says all the girls at school have crushes on him because he has such big muscles, but I didn't think he was cute at all. Ross Perlman is cute. Mr. Calegari looks like a gym teacher.

Mom and Mr. Calegari went to dinner and a movie together, and they saw *Love Circle* rated R and I made a point of being awake when they got back (I was hiding in my bedroom) and I could hear them talking about what a "sensuous" movie it was. I thought that meant full of senses, but I looked it up in the dictionary this morning, and it means sexy, so I guess that was why the movie was rated R. I bet it had curse words in it too.

Judy lives in the apartment complex, so Mr. Calegari didn't have to drive her home. I opened my door just a little after she left, and listened to Mom and Mr. Calegari discuss what a sensuous movie they had seen and how delicious dinner had been, and then they kissed. I could hear them, but just to be on the safe side, I peeked, and they were kissing. Then Mom giggled some more and said she was out of practice and Mr. Calegari said it was just like riding a bicycle, whatever that means, because as far as I can see kissing and riding a bike have absolutely nothing in common. I think he has muscles for brains. Anyway, Mom smiled at that, and then she kissed him, and it didn't look to me like she was out of practice. I thought it was disgusting, so I stopped looking before they turned the living room into an R-rated movie. He left a couple of minutes later; I could hear him go out, and the minute he was out the door, Mom called Sheila and she must have been on the phone for as long as the date had lasted. I guess she was giving her a blow-by-blow account of every muscle.

This morning Mom asked me all nice and casual how my evening had been and what did I think of Mr. Calegari and wasn't he nice and handsome and he thought I was terrific, so bright and nicely mannered and I just grunted. I wasn't about to tell her I thought he was ugly and stupid even though he was. Mom's smart enough to figure that out for herself eventually.

Then Mom said, "In my divorce books it said sometimes the children resent it when the mother starts dating again and I guess this is one of those times," so I said I didn't resent it at all, she could go out with Frankenstein for all I cared and then I ran to my room and slammed my door real loud. Mom thinks the whole world is in those divorce books, which just goes to show how wrong she can be. I don't resent it that Mom went out with Mr. Calegari. I didn't resent it when you told Nana you were dating too. I know the two of you are never going to get remarried. I know you used to fight all the time. I know you live in Missouri so it isn't like you can take Mom out to dinner and the movies on Saturday night even if you wanted to, and I know you don't. I just think Mr. Calegari is all wrong for Mom and someday she'll realize it and then she'll be sorry.

I'd tell you all the stuff that happened to me in school this week but I felt this was more important. You should know that Mom is making a total fool of herself over some muscle-bound jerk so you can tell me what to do.

Love,
Laurie

January 30

Dear Dad,

I got your letter yesterday, and I really thought it was stupid. What do you mean it's none of your concern if Mom is dating again? Of course it's your concern. You were her husband for years and years, and you're my father, and that makes you very concerned.

And I didn't understand the part about how I should leave Mom alone and let her go out with whoever she wants. I didn't stop her. I didn't even tell her I felt sick, even though I had a terrible stomachache.

She's going out with Mr. Calegari again tonight, and the way I see it, it serves both of you right.

Love,
Laurie

P.S. Someday I'm going to go out with a guy and you and Mom will both hate him, and I'll say, "What do I care, you both dated people I didn't like one bit and that never stopped you," and then you'll see how it feels.

February 4

Dear Dad,

I know I'm going to spend part of Washington's birthday week with you, but do you think we could talk about my living with you for good while I'm out there? I think I'd be a lot happier in Missouri, and I promise I won't be too much of a bother once I'm there.

Love,
Laurie

February 5

Dear Dad,

Mom and I had the worst fight we ever had after school, and I hate her and I hate living here and I just have to move to Missouri. I promise I'll be good. Just let me stay with you.

Love,
Laurie

February 6

Dear Dad,

Mom is out with Bruno again tonight, and Judy my stupid babysitter is on the phone with her boyfriend, so I figured I'd better write to you and explain about how horrible things are here, so you can see that I should stay with you in Missouri once I fly out there next week.

You know Mom's been seeing this stupid Bruno person on Saturday nights, and now she's also seeing him on Wednesdays, although I don't see why, since they work at the same school and can see each other every day if they want.

Anyway, on Wednesday, Mom said, "Bruno and I are going out for supper tonight — nothing fancy — probably just a pizza, would you like to come with us?" She asked it real fast, just like I wrote it, and her face was kind of flushed, and she smiled a lot.

So I said no, I didn't want to join them, because I didn't and besides I had two tests on Friday, one in math and one in French, and it seems to me Mom never lets me do anything on school nights so why should this be different? And Mom said it was different, and we wouldn't be out late at all, and she didn't know where she was going to find a babysitter for me on such short notice, and I said that was why she wanted me to go with them, so she wouldn't have to pay for a babysitter, and she said I was turning into a real brat and I said how would she know since she was never around anymore and

80

when she was, she was always on the phone with Sheila telling her about Bruno this and Bruno that.

Then Mom said, "I don't care how you feel about Bruno, he's been very nice to you, and wants you to like him, but it doesn't matter to me one way or the other, because I like him a lot, and that's all that counts." And I said, "I thought I was what counted," and Mom said, "Of course you are, but I'm entitled to a little happiness too, and Bruno makes me happy."

So I said, "Daddy used to make you happy and see how that turned out," and Mom said, "This is no time to discuss your father and me and besides, we both have to get to school, so I guess I'll just have to tell Bruno some other time, but don't think you've heard the last of this."

That afternoon, I went straight to my room and hid in there, in case Mom had changed her mind and Bruno was going to come over after all, but he didn't, and after a while I came out, but we didn't talk much.

Then Thursday evening, the doorbell rang, and I answered it, and it was Bruno carrying a pizza box, and he said, "Pizza man with mushrooms and onions," and I swear Daddy just the smell of the pizza made me sick to my stomach, and I ran to my room, because otherwise I would have thrown up all over him, and Mom would have hated me for doing that. So by staying in my room all evening, I was really being nice, only Mom didn't see it that way, and Friday morning she screamed at me. Her face was bright red and she said I was the rudest creature she'd ever met and the cruelest and Bruno had done nothing to deserve this kind of behavior, and she wanted me to love you because you were my father, but I had to get all these romantic notions out of my head about the two of you and realize that you both had your own lives to lead and right now hers included Bruno whether I liked it or not.

Daddy, I don't have any romantic notions about you and her, you know that, but I said, "I heard you crying when I told you Daddy was going out again, so I guess you're the one with the romantic notions," and Mom said, "Of course it hurt when I realized your father was dating other women, but then I decided he was right, and I should be dating, too, and Bruno asked me out months earlier, but I had said no, so I went up to him and asked him if he was still interested, and fortunately for me, he was, and I wish you'd give him a break and then you'd see what a nice man he is, smart and funny, and he has two kids of his own and he likes kids and he'd really like to get to know you better."

So I said, "He wouldn't like to know me if I'm throwing up all over him," because that was what I was afraid I was going to do the night before, only Mom misunderstood, and she screamed at me some more for threatening to throw up on him, which wasn't what I meant at all, but I couldn't make her understand. By then we were both crying, and we both had to get to school, and Mom said since I liked staying in my room so much, I was grounded for the whole weekend, and could spend it in my room thinking about how nasty I'd become and when I was ready to apologize to her and to Bruno, I could open the door, come on out, and they'd be happy to see what a real human being looked like.

At lunch I almost asked Kris if I could spend the

weekend at her house, but I realized Mom would really kill me if I went there without her permission, so I went back home, and went straight to my room, and closed the door, and even when Mom told me to come out for supper, I refused. So she came into my room with my supper, which I hadn't asked her to do, and she said she was sorry she had shouted at me that morning but I was driving her crazy and if I could at least tell her what it was I didn't like about Bruno, maybe we could have a rational discussion about it.

I had the funniest thought then, Dad. I remembered Mrs. Coleman asking me why I wanted to be in the gifted and talented program, and how I couldn't think why, I just knew I wanted it. I felt that way about Bruno. He really has been very nice to me when we've met. He shakes my hand, and asks me how school is, and he laughs when I say something dumb, but it isn't a mean laugh. It's like he decided what I said was actually a joke, and not dumb, and that's why he's laughing. And it isn't his fault he has an ugly name and all those muscles. So I didn't say anything.

That was a big mistake. Mom got all smiley then, and said, "I knew you really liked him, and how about if tomorrow we all do something together?" and I said, "I'd rather die." So Mom got mad at me again, and I guess I got really angry, too, because I picked up my supper plate and I threw it across the room, and it smashed against the wall and all the food went flying. Mom got real mad then and she said I was selfish and rotten and didn't care about anybody except myself, and I said that was twice as true for her and if she really loved me she'd stop seeing Bruno and she said, "Don't you ever make demands like that to me again," and she told me I had to clean up my room and if I thought the best thing to do with food was waste it, then I could just see what feeling hungry was like and skip supper altogether. So I said the way she cooked, I'd rather be hungry, only she'd run out of the room by then, and I could hear her pick up the phone and call someone. I don't know whether it was Sheila or Bruno or Gran. Whoever she called though, she was crying, and I was glad, because I was crying too, because I always thought Mom loved me and now I know she doesn't.

Daddy, you can go out with whoever you want, if you just let me stay in Missouri. I hate Mom and she hates me and if you were still living here with us then it would be different, but if you're going to live a thousand miles away, then the least you can do is let me live there with you.

I promise I'll be the best daughter ever if you just let me stay with you.

Love,
Laurie

P.S. If you want, you can call Mom and read her every single word in this letter so she can see how much I hate her and how much I want to live with you.

February 7

Dear Dad,

I told Mom I wanted to live with you, and she said, "I'll just bet you do, but you don't solve a problem by running away from it." So I said there wasn't any problem, she wanted to be with Bruno, and it would be easier for her if I lived far away. Mom said yes, she did like Bruno, but Bruno wasn't the issue, because she doubted she was going to marry Bruno, so after a while she'd probably stop dating him and start dating somebody else, and was I going to keep sulking and throwing food dishes around every time she had a date? If I was, she'd switch to paper plates.

So I thought about throwing paper plates across the room, and I giggled. And Mom giggled too, and then we stopped giggling and we both laughed, and I guess we hugged then, and kissed, and I said, "You're really not going to marry Bruno?"

And Mom said, "I don't think so, honey, but I would like to marry somebody someday, and I could wait until you're off in college, but that won't be for another seven years, and if I find somebody before then, I have to know that you're not going to break all the good china."

So I said, "It scared me that you dated Bruno," and Mom said, "It scared me too, because for the first time I realized my marriage to your father was truly over, and that hurts, but it's time for me to move on with my life, and that means going out with different men. Bruno was the first, but I hope he won't be the last. You're going to have to learn to live with that."

"What if I honestly don't like one of them?" I said. "What if one of them is mean to me or I know he has two wives and six children or he tries to kiss me?"

"Then you tell me immediately," Mom said. "And I'll dump him so fast it'll make your head spin."

I guess we hugged and kissed some more. Mom said, "You're going to be a teenager soon, and if you're anything like I was, you're going to make my life miserable, because I certainly made my mom's life miserable when I was a teenager." So I asked her what she had done, but she refused to tell me. "I'll just make sure to buy plenty of paper plates," she said instead.

I feel a lot better about things, now that Mom and I have talked. I'm still real glad I'm going to be seeing you next week, but I don't feel like I have to live with you anymore. I hope you don't mind.

Love,
Laurie

P.S. Could we eat Mexican food while I'm visiting? Mom hates Mexican food, so I never get to eat any here.

February 21

Dear Dad,
I had a wonderful visit with you and thank you for letting me eat Mexican food for dinner three

nights in a row, even if it did give me a stomachache.

Mom said she had lunch with Bruno and his children one day while I was in Missouri, and that both his children were total brats. She says she's very glad he doesn't have custody, and even so, she's glad she has no intention of ever marrying him. But he's coming over Wednesday anyway, and we're all going to have pizza and watch a video of something together. I hope Bruno brings the tape of *Temptation*, which is rated R, so Mom won't take it out for us.

Also while I was in Missouri, I got a phone call from Jamie. Remember Jamie? She was the one who screamed all during my sleepover. I haven't called her back yet, since I don't know what to say to her.

I'd better stop writing now, and finish all my homework I didn't do while I was with you.

Love,
Laurie

February 28

Dear Dad,

Usually I write to you on weekends, mostly on Saturdays, but sometimes on Sunday, and today I'm writing to you on Sunday, but it's real late, much later than I usually write. Want to know why? Because I was at Jamie's for a sleepover last night.

I bet you're surprised. I'm pretty surprised too. Jamie called me while I was in Missouri and Mom took the message, but I didn't call her back until Tuesday, because I didn't know what to say to her when I did call. She was so horrible at my sleepover. Everybody was horrible, but she was the worst. Mom said I didn't even have to call her back as far as she was concerned, because Jamie had been so horrible. Mom said she still gets a headache whenever she thinks about Jamie screaming, and she wasn't even with us when Jamie was screaming while we trick-or-treated.

But I was curious about why Jamie had called, so Tuesday after supper I called her. She had just finished her supper too, so I guess her family eats supper the same time Mom and I do.

Before I practically had a chance to say anything, Jamie apologized to me. She said she knew she'd behaved badly at my sleepover, and she'd wanted to apologize to me for a while now, but she'd been too shy. Can you believe anybody who could scream that loud could be shy about anything?

So I told her she really had been awful, and she said she knew she had, that she never behaved that way, and it's true, when we were in camp together, she always acted like she was sane, and she said sometimes when she was nervous about things she acted like a total idiot, which was how she had acted at my sleepover. So I asked her what she was nervous about, and she said that she knew Kris was my best friend, and Shannon was my second best friend, and Darin was my best friend at camp, and that just made her my second best at camp friend, which wasn't very much, and she didn't know about Kris and Shannon, but Darin was so much smarter than she was, and prettier, and she figured since

Kris was in the gifted and talented program then she had to be smart too, and she bet Shannon was pretty wonderful also, and so was I, and that meant she was going to come in fifth, and her mother first said she couldn't have any sweets at all and then her mother said she could have a small piece of birthday cake but that was it, and then her mother said she could have two pieces of candy and a small piece of birthday cake, and then her mother said she didn't give a damn how much garbage Jamie ate, just as long as Jamie knew she was going to be a raving loony from eating it, so Jamie kept expecting to be a raving loony and sure enough she was one. It seems to me she was one before she ate any of the candy, but maybe my memory is off.

Then Jamie said that it had been real weird seeing me not in summer camp, and it wasn't like she saw Darin either, so everything felt weird and everybody else was as wonderful and perfect as she'd thought they'd be (believe me, Dad, Shannon was anything but wonderful and perfect) and she ended up acting like a total fool and she hated herself for the way she behaved, and could I ever forgive her.

So I thought about it, because that sleepover was practically the worst thing that ever happened to me in my life, and I realized I'd forgiven Shannon and she'd been terrible, and I'd forgiven Darin, and I'd forgiven Kris, and I'd forgiven you for cancelling out at Thanksgiving, and I'd forgiven Mom for dating Bruno (even though he didn't bring *Temptation*, he brought a stupid Disney movie instead), and I'd forgiven Jimmy and I'd even forgiven Mrs. Coleman for not putting me in the gifted and talented program and not knowing my name. I've done a lot of forgiving this year. That meant the only person I hadn't forgiven was Jamie, and to be perfectly honest, I'd hardly thought about her at all lately, which is why I hadn't forgiven her.

So I forgave her. I told her sometimes I act like a raving loony myself, and that two weeks ago, I'd thrown my supper plate clear across the room and broken the plate and there'd been mashed potatoes and peas all over the floor. And Jamie said, "smashed potatoes," and that was so funny we just started laughing, and I remembered why I'd liked her in summer camp, which was because she said so many funny things.

So after we stopped laughing she asked what was new, and I told her, and so much has happened it practically took forever, and she told me what was new with her, which wasn't quite as interesting as what was new with me, but that's because her mother, who's divorced too, isn't seeing anybody right now, so I told her all about Bruno, and Jamie said her mother would like to date someone with a really great body too.

Then Jamie said if I'd truly forgiven her and we were speaking again, would I like to come over to her house this weekend for a sleepover? She said she was going to invite Darin too, and it would just be the three of us and she promised she wouldn't scream once, not even if Darin and I threw frogs and snakes on her. And for a moment, I wasn't sure, because I thought maybe I should go over there and be as rotten to her as she'd been to me, but that seemed so mean I thought maybe I shouldn't go at all, and then I thought maybe I should go and just have a good time, so I said yes if Mom agreed, and Jamie held on while I asked Mom, and Mom said, "Just as long as I don't have to listen to her," which I figured meant yes.

So yesterday, Mom drove me to Jamie's, which is over an hour away, and when we got there, Jamie's mother had made lunch for all of us, which Mom agreed was an extremely nice thing of her to do, and the two of them sat around discussing being divorced and raising crazy daughters, and they liked each other so much I was worried Mom might join the sleepover, except she had a date with Bruno that night, so she had to get home and try on all her dresses. When she described all of Bruno's muscles, she and Jamie's mother laughed dirty, which was really kind of interesting.

Then right before Mom left, Darin came, and Mom got to say hello and goodbye to her too, and then Darin and Jamie and I went to Jamie's room, which is very pretty and has a patchwork quilt Jamie's grandmother made for her when she was born and we looked at magazines and talked about boys. I guess we talked about other stuff too, like school, but we all go to different schools, so it was hard to talk about that, but even though we all know different boys, we had plenty to say about them.

Then Jamie's mom took us out to a Chinese restaurant for supper, and Jamie knows how to use chopsticks, so Darin and I tried to learn how, only we kept dropping our food on our laps, and Jamie made us laugh by telling us to eat our soup with chopsticks. After a while Darin went back to a fork, but I kept on trying with the chopsticks. I got pretty good at them too, but the rice was still tricky. Next time I see you, let's eat at a Chinese restaurant and you can see how well I do.

After supper, Jamie's mom took us to an ice-cream parlor and we all got big sundaes, even Jamie. I got hot fudge with fudge-ripple ice cream and whipped cream. It came with a long, skinny spoon, and Jamie's mom said, "I always wished I had a figure like this spoon but I guess as long as I eat sundaes I never will," and we all laughed. Jamie looks a lot like her mother, and she sounds like her too, but when I told Jamie that, she just made a face and said she wished she was nothing like her mother or her father too for that matter, she wished she was an orphan. She said all that after we got back to her home, and we were alone in her bedroom where her mother couldn't hear her. Darin said she liked her parents, although she wished her mother wouldn't nag so much, and her father worried too much about her, and always checked her homework. Jamie said her father never checked her homework even when he was still living at home because he was always chasing women, and now he had remarried and lived someplace else and her mom says he's probably still chasing women because men like that never change.

So then I guess I complained about you and Mom because I had to. I didn't want Darin and Jamie to think I had perfect parents, because they'd get jealous. And then we danced. Jamie knows all the new dances, so she taught them to us, and we talked some more, and we didn't go to bed until way past two, and we never even turned the TV set on once.

Today we slept late, and when we woke up Jamie's mother made us waffles. She said she'd had the waffle iron since she got married and this was the first time she'd used it, and she burnt the first couple, but then she got the hang of it, and we all had waffles. Mom came over around twelve, and she and Jamie's mother had coffee, and then Darin's mother came, and she had coffee too, and Darin and I both wanted to get going because we had homework to do, only the three mothers were having such a good time we thought they'd never leave. It was pretty funny. Jamie's mom kept saying, "You girls were up until two in the morning talking last night, why don't you just keep talking about what you were talking about last night while I visit with your mothers?" only we couldn't because we'd been talking about how awful our mothers are and about boys, and we couldn't talk about stuff like that while our mothers were there. It ended up that Mom and Jamie's mom decided they'd get together someday for lunch and if Jamie and I wanted to visit then fine, and if not, then we'd just entertain ourselves some other way. I think Mom wants to tell Jamie's mom some more about Bruno's muscles.

When I finally got home, I had all that homework to do, which I hadn't done all weekend, even though Mom told me to do it on Friday. I hate doing homework on Friday. That's why it's taken me so long to write to you, although I guess you couldn't tell whether I wrote this letter first thing in the morning or last thing at night, since you'd get it the same time no matter when I wrote it.

Mom just knocked on my door to see what I was doing and when I told her I was writing to you, she said, "Don't forget to tell your father about how you're doing in school," so I got a 92 in my last French test, and an 88 in math and a Very Good Plus on my last English composition. I didn't do so good in my science test, I got a 79, but I should have gotten higher, only I wasn't thinking. That happens sometimes. Mom said so, after she said, "Couldn't you at least have gotten an 80, which is so much more respectable than a 79?" Only I guess I couldn't, because I didn't. I told her I'd do better next time, and she said she was sure I would.

In spite of my 79, basically I am very happy, and like having Jamie as a friend again (she's so nice when she isn't screaming) and if I don't stop this letter right away, I won't get any sleep and then my grades will really be terrible at school.

Love,
Laurie

P.S. Mom's birthday is in two weeks, and I don't know what to get her. Sometimes I think I should get her something pretty, but other times I think I should just get her a book or a new teapot. This is a very hard decision.

March 5

Dear Dad,

I had such a good time last weekend and on Monday I got a letter from Victoria Rosamond James and Kris and I had lunch together and I got to tell her all about the great time I had at the sleepover, and I knew she was jealous because she has to spend her summers in Indiana and doesn't get to go to summer camp and make different friends.

But Tuesday and Wednesday were awful and Mom and I were both in bad moods. Mom says it's because it's March, and even though her birthday is in March, she hates March because it's such a dreary ugly month and February is bad too but you expect it to be bad and you just want March to be perfect because it isn't February. Mom said I shouldn't bother to write all that to you, because she used to say it to you every March so you already know how she feels, but I thought you might like to know her feelings haven't changed.

Bruno was supposed to come over on Wednesday night, but it snowed instead, and that made Mom mad too, not that she blamed him, but she was disappointed. Only it kept on snowing (it wasn't supposed to, the weather reports said maybe two inches only we had six instead) and we had a snow day on Thursday, which Mom and I agreed was exactly what the whole world needed. Not like we made snowmen like we did the last snow day. Mom spent the day doing paperwork, and I worked on my report for social studies (now that we're through the states, we're studying all the countries in South America and I have to write a report on Ecuador, which is on the equator, which is about the only interesting thing you can say about it). It was really nice. Everything outside was so pretty, and other people made snowmen, without us having to tell them to, and Mom made hot chocolate for us and she baked bread, which she hasn't done in ages, and the apartment smelled great, and the bread tasted delicious too. Mom was worried because the yeast was so old, but the bread rose just fine.

That night Bruno came over, and Mom had baked the bread, so she made a really nice supper and we ate at the table and she put candles on it and everything, so it wasn't pizza on the floor, like we usually have. It felt nice sitting around the table, eating grown-up food. That was what Mom called it.

Even though we all had school the next day, it wasn't nearly so bad because we had the day off on Thursday. And when Mom was in the bathroom, Bruno asked me what he should get her for her birthday, which I thought was really nice of him, even though I don't know what I'm getting her myself. I don't think it matters what Bruno gets her, I think Mom is going to be happy just getting something from him. I think Mom likes Bruno a lot more than she's willing to admit, and if his children weren't brats, maybe she'd want to marry him after all.

Jamie hates her stepmother and her stepbrothers, but she doesn't have a stepfather so I don't know if she'd hate him, too. Do you think you might get married again? If you did, would I still be able to see you? All this is very confusing, but I don't think I'll worry about it just now. Not while I have this paper on Ecuador to write.

Love,
Laurie

P.S. Are you going to get Mom a birthday present too? Jamie said her father would never get her mother anything, but I know you really sent her that fudge and not me.

March 13

Dear Dad,

Friday was Mom's birthday and up until Thursday I didn't know what to get her. There was this book I knew she wanted to read, and she's been saying she wanted a new teapot but I felt weird going into a store to buy a teapot, and when I went into the bookstore to buy the book, it turned out to cost $15.95 plus tax, which was more than I had on me or was likely to have on me for the next two years. Mom says I spend my money too fast, but the way I see it, I don't have that much money, so naturally I spend it fast.

What I had was seven dollars plus enough change to cover sales tax and I thought about getting Mom an expensive paperback but I didn't want to do that either. I saw some pretty stationery, but I'm the one who always writes the letters, not Mom, so I didn't think she'd get that much use out of it.

I was at the Ten Oaks Mall because that's the one closest to home, and I went into the gift shop there, but there was nothing I liked for Mom that I could afford to buy, so I went into the drugstore to see if the new issue of *Teen Dreamboat* was out (it wasn't), and I saw all these pretty bottles of perfume. They weren't perfume really, just cologne,

97

but the prettiest bottle cost $6.95, which with my extra change was just what I could afford. I don't know how it smelled, because when I sprayed the colognes around, they all smelled the same to me, but the bottle was so pretty. It had little roses painted on it and the perfume was called Rosa, which I liked because it reminded me of Victoria Rosamond James. So I bought it. They wouldn't gift wrap it for me because they said they were a drugstore, but I went home, and looked around, and found some wrapping paper and wrapped it myself. Then I went to the box where Mom keeps her spare change and took some out and bought her a birthday card with it (I only took fifty cents; I still had fifty cents of my own).

Friday morning, I got up before Mom did, and I put up her coffee and made her French toast, which is her favorite thing that I know how to make, and when she got out of the shower, her breakfast was waiting for her, and I put her present and card on the table by her plate. And she loved them, Dad. She put the cologne on right at the table, and she kept sniffing herself until she left for school, and when she read the birthday card I got her, she hugged me. I'd found a birthday candle which I kind of propped up on her French toast, and I sang "Happy Birthday" to her and she blew out the candle and hugged me some more. That night, she and Bruno had a special date because it was her birthday and he took her out to dinner and gave her a pin. It's pretty, too. I spent the night at Kris's, which was why I made her birthday celebration for breakfast, when I knew I'd be seeing her.

Mom said it was the nicest birthday she ever had,

although I think she's wrong, since I remember the birthday she had when you were still married and you went away for the weekend to that inn and Mom said it was the most beautiful place she'd ever been to. I don't know. Maybe that was the most beautiful birthday she ever had, and this one was the nicest. In any event, she was happy, and that made me happy. I also had a very good time at Kris's. It's fun being there because she still has both parents, and it's nice seeing a father and a mother, even though her kid brother is a brat. Kris says when he was born she really liked the idea of having a baby brother, but now that he's been around for a while, she knows it was a big mistake.

If Mom marries Bruno or somebody else, then I might end up with a baby brother or sister. That would be so weird. Of course it would be weird just having a stepfather. It's really a lot easier when mothers and fathers just stay married the way they're supposed to.

Love,
Laurie

P.S. Not that I'm complaining.

March 19

Dear Dad,
You know how Jimmy and I are friends again, even though we hardly talk? Well, yesterday after

school, he kind of grabbed me and pulled me to the side of the school where the other kids might not see us, and asked me if I wanted to come over to his house sometime, the way I used to.

"Not if you grab me like that," I said.

So Jimmy apologized. He said he didn't want Joe Malone to know he was asking me, and I said if he didn't want Joe Malone to know then I didn't want to go, because I wasn't going to go sneaking around just so Joe Malone wouldn't get upset. Then Jimmy said the reason Joe Malone would get upset was because Joe Malone told him he thought I wasn't ugly. I said I certainly wasn't ugly, but Joe Malone could stand a nose job or two. Jimmy said when Joe Malone said a girl wasn't ugly what he meant was she was pretty and he liked her. Which is probably the dumbest thing I ever heard.

I said if Joe Malone thinks I'm pretty and he likes me (and believe me, Dad, he's never once said anything nicer to me than "Get out of my way, snotbrain"), why should he be upset if I visited Jimmy? Jimmy said Joe Malone would be jealous and think Jimmy was making time with me when he wanted to and then Joe Malone might beat Jimmy up. But he wouldn't grab me anymore.

Mom says boys get weird around this age, and when I went home and told her all this she said it was just about springtime and that got their juices rising. It doesn't feel like springtime, since the weather's been cold all week and we even had a snow flurry today. And I don't see why boys' juices should get rising in the middle of March and not girls', although frankly it would take a lot more than Joe Malone to get my juices rising. My puke

100

rising maybe, but not my juices. Which I told Mom. She said she thought Joe Malone was kind of cute, or at least he had been two years ago, which was the last birthday party of mine I'd invited him to.

Then Mom said I was a very pretty girl and lots of boys were going to like me, and she guessed it had already started, but since she wasn't going to let me date until I was at least 25, she refused to worry. So I said she'd been married before she was 25, and she said that was the problem. "I won't let you make that mistake," was what she actually said, which probably has something to do with you. I finally bargained her down to 23.

After we had our talk, I went to the mirror and looked at myself to see if I really was pretty. I don't know. I think Shannon is prettier than me, and Darin, and Victoria Rosamond James (she sent me a picture). I'm as pretty as Kris, I think, and Maria, and I think I'm prettier than Jamie (don't tell her I said that). And I think we're all a lot better looking than Joe Malone.

Mom's been looking prettier since she started dating Bruno. She wears her hair a little differently and the Rosa Cologne I got her really smells nice.

Meanwhile something interesting is going to happen at school. This famous writer is coming to talk. Her name is Liz Reuben, and I've actually read a couple of her books, even before I knew she was coming. She's pretty good (but I like Ellen Conford better. Also Paula Danziger). She's going to talk to all the sixth-graders, not just the gifted and talented ones. When I first heard she was coming, I was afraid she was only going to talk to the gifted and talented students, but instead she's talking to all the sixth-graders, no matter how ungifted and untalented we are. Only she's going to have lunch with the gifted and talented students, which means Kris is going to have lunch with her. Kris is real excited, because Liz Reuben is her favorite writer, and she's read five of her books. I guess I'm happy for her.

Mr. Rodriguez said we each had to read at least one book by Liz Reuben, only I don't know if he means one we haven't read, or if we've already read two we don't have to read any. He didn't explain. He also said we should come up with questions we want to ask her, since she likes answering questions. She'll autograph our books too, if we want.

I have never met a famous writer before. If you don't count Mickey Mouse at Disney World, I have never met a famous person before, and I don't think you should count Mickey Mouse, because even if he is famous, he isn't a person. Maybe Bruno was a famous wrestler, but I don't think so. So when I get Liz Reuben's autograph, she'll be the first famous person I've ever really spoken to.

I wonder if she has good handwriting.

Love,
Laurie

P.S. I have this kind of dream that I ask Liz Reuben the most wonderful question she's ever been asked, and she's so impressed that she finds Mrs. Coleman and tells her she has to put me in the gifted and talented program. I know it's too late for me to do anything with it this year, but they must be selecting kids for next year, and I don't think I've made enough of an impression on Mrs. Coleman that she'll put me in without someone telling her to.

She'd have to if someone famous asked her, don't you think?

March 27

Dear Dad,

Liz Reuben is coming to talk on April 14, and just to be extra gifted and talented, I've read four of her books in the past week. That way I've read even more than Kris, so I figure the questions I ask her will really stand out.

The problem is I've been so busy reading her books, I haven't had time to think of any questions. Also I haven't done much homework. I've been doing what I have to, but I haven't been studying the way I usually do, and I had a science test this week I don't think I did real well on. I had a spelling test and I got four words wrong, and Mr. Rodriguez wrote a note on it saying, "You always do better than this," which was nice of him to notice. I almost never spell anything wrong. You may have noticed that too.

I did get an 88 on my math test though, which is very good for me. And Joe Malone made kissy noises at me when I was on line in the cafeteria. I was standing with Shannon and she made kissy noises back.

Maybe I should ask Liz Reuben if anybody ever made kissy noises at her.

Love,
Laurie

P.S. I asked Mom about the kissy noises, and she said while she understood that I wanted to ask Liz Reuben a truly wonderful question no one had ever asked her before, she didn't think that was it. "Try something a little less personal," she said.

So I asked Mom if Bruno made kissy noises at her at school, and she said no, they tried to act like they weren't even dating at school, even though everybody at school knows they are. She said it wouldn't look right to the students if they saw two of their teachers kissing in the hallway but frankly I think I'd like it if I saw two of my teachers kissing. Mr. Rodriguez is very cute and I think he's dating Ms. Antonelli, who teaches eighth-grade English. If I saw them kissing, then I'd know for sure.

P.P.S. I'll see you next week for spring vacation. Mom wants to know if the weather is warm already in Missouri or if she should pack my winter stuff.

April 16

Dear Dad,

Liz Reuben came to school on Thursday, and it was pretty interesting.

It turned out she wasn't just talking with the sixth-graders. She talked with the seventh-graders too, and Mrs. Coleman's class was there with my class and Ms. Taylor's class. It was pretty crowded in the library with all of us there, but we sat on the floor, and Liz Reuben talked pretty loud.

As soon as I saw Mrs. Coleman I knew all I had to do was ask a couple of truly wonderful questions and that would prove to her then and there how gifted and talented I was. Kris thought so too. She really elbowed me when she saw Mrs. Coleman's class walk in.

Liz Reuben talked a little bit about herself, and then she asked us for questions. At first nobody had any questions to ask, but then somebody asked something, and pretty soon we were all asking questions.

I asked a question too. I'd been working all week on finding just the perfect question, but I never really found one I loved completely. Think about it, how hard it is to come up with just the right question, something brilliant but not too personal. And knowing Mrs. Coleman was there made me even more nervous.

Actually I don't think I would have asked anything except Kris elbowed me again. So I asked Liz Reuben if she ever hated any of her titles. She laughed, and said nobody had ever asked her that, at least not that way, and yes, there were a couple of titles of her books she hadn't named that she wasn't real crazy about. So it was a good question, but I didn't think it was such a great question that Mrs. Coleman was instantly going to put me in the gifted and talented program.

After I asked my question, something kind of interesting happened. Liz Reuben asked us a question. She asked us who Dale Baker was.

None of us students knew, and it turned out the teachers didn't know either. Mr. Rodriguez said he thought Dale Baker was a principal once, but Mrs.

Coleman said she thought Dale Baker had been mayor of the town when the school was built. Liz Reuben said she thought it was pretty strange that we were all spending five days a week in a building named for someone we didn't know who it was. She said she lived in a town named Middletown, and everybody knew it was in the middle and that's why it was called Middletown.

So Mrs. Coleman explained that we didn't used to be the Dale Baker Middle School, we used to be the Dale Baker Junior High School, and there was a plaque in the hallway that said who Dale Baker was, but when they changed it to a middle school they did some renovations, and the plaque must have disappeared. Not that she'd ever read it, but she was sure somebody in the main office would remember who Dale Baker was.

Then Mr. Rodriguez said for the first two years he'd taught there, he thought it was the Dave Baker school, because everybody just calls it Baker, and somehow he got it in his head that it was Dave and not Dale. And Liz Reuben said when your last name is Reuben you're always very careful about other people's names, spelling and pronouncing them right, which makes sense because Mrs. Jay, who's the librarian, misspelt Reuben on her Welcome Liz Reuben banner.

Mrs. Coleman said she was very embarrassed not to know who Dale Baker was, and I was glad to see her embarrassed because I always feel embarrassed when I talk with her. Liz Reuben said it was funny that none of us knew, but when she got home, she'd check on Middletown, because maybe it wasn't in the middle after all, and they were lying when they named it that.

It's probably mean of me to be glad that Mrs. Coleman didn't know something, but since I haven't thought she was all that gifted and talented since she couldn't remember my name I was glad everybody else could see her that way. I don't think anybody but me cared, but that's okay too.

Love,
Laurie

P.S. I just remembered the really good thing that happened with Liz Reuben. Some kid asked her who her favorite writer was, and she said Emily Brontë, and I got all excited and said she lived in Haworth, and that was the town next to Keighly, where my pen pal lives. And Liz Reuben said she'd taken the train to Keighly once, and walked from there to Haworth, and it was very pretty countryside, but the walk was long and straight uphill. I looked over at Mrs. Coleman then to see if she was impressed, but she was whispering something to Mrs. Jay, so I don't think she heard.

P.P.S. Kris got to have lunch with Liz Reuben because she's in the gifted and talented program. She said I didn't miss much. She said Liz Reuben ate a lot and didn't have great table manners and talked with her mouth full.

P.P.P.S. Did I tell you I had a wonderful time in Missouri? I did. I can't wait until summer! ! !

Dear Dad,

I just had an idea that is so brilliant I'm going to write to you even though it's the middle of the week and I already wrote you a couple of days ago.

I'm going to find out who Dale Baker is and then I'll tell Mrs. Coleman and she'll see how gifted and talented I truly am.

Love,
Laurie

P.S. I told Mom my idea, and she agreed it was brilliant.

April 23

Dear Dad,

Remember how I told you I was going to find out who Dale Baker was? Well the next day, I went to the public library and said, "I go to the Dale Baker Middle School, and I want to know who Dale Baker is." The reference librarian said that made sense to her, and it would be interesting to know (she said she just moved to town that winter, and she had no idea who Dale Baker might be).

So she asked if anybody in the library knew how old the Dale Baker Middle School was, and I said it used to be the Dale Baker Junior High School, and one of the library clerks said she'd gone to school there when it had been the junior high, and that had been twenty years ago, but her older brother who was five years older had gone to the old junior high, so the school must be around twenty-two years old.

The reference librarian said it must have made the newspapers when the school was dedicated, and all the old newspapers were on microfilm, so she found the right year, and set the machine up, and I looked through all those old newspapers real small until I found the right date. It turned out that Dale Baker was the first superintendent of schools in our district.

Frankly Dad, I was disappointed, although I did like the idea that someday they might name a school for you if you ever get promoted. Dale Baker was alive when they named our school for him, and there was a picture of him. He looked old but pretty healthy. The reference librarian asked me if I wanted a copy of the article so I would always know who Dale Baker was, and first I thought no, but then I said yes. I wasn't sure what I was going to do with it, since Dale Baker turned out to be such a boring person, but I figured I might as well.

So the librarian made the copy, and while she was doing that another librarian walked in, and the reference librarian told him what she was doing, and the other librarian said he was friends with Dale Baker's son Mark, and he'd been to Dale Baker's funeral which was about ten years ago.

So the reference librarian asked me if I wanted to find his obituary, which would have a lot more information on Dale Baker, and I said yes, and she got out the microfilm and I looked at all the miniature papers until I found him. He was eighty-two when he died and he left a widow and two sons and four grandchildren, in case you want to know. The librarian made a copy of the obituary for me, and when I left the library I felt like even if I wasn't the only person in town who knew who Dale Baker was, I certainly was the only one at the Dale Baker School who knew.

I showed Mom the article and the obituary when I got home and she agreed with me that while Dale Baker was obviously a very fine person and deserved to have a school named after him, he wasn't the most exciting person she'd ever heard of. "He didn't exactly climb Mount Everest," was how she put it.

But I still figured Mrs. Coleman would be impressed that I went to the bother to find out, and besides, she'd said gifted and talented people talk about other people, and that was what I was doing, talking about someone who wasn't me. So I took all the information I had and wrote a little report about Dale Baker, and I cut out the picture of him and Scotch-taped it to the bottom of the report. I showed it to Mom when I finished it.

You know that look Mom gets when you do something exactly right but she's disappointed anyway? That's what she looked like. And that's what I felt like. I'd written a perfectly okay report about Dale Baker, which is more than anybody else probably thought to do, and I could show it to Mrs. Coleman and she'd see I could find something out for myself without anybody assigning it to me and that might be enough to make her put me in the gifted and talented program, but I wanted something more.

"It's a shame Dale Baker was so dull," Mom said.

So the next day I didn't show the report to Mrs. Coleman the way I planned to. I took it to school, but I didn't stay late. I went home instead and I read the report, and I thought about Dale Baker and what a boring person he turned out to be and how disappointed Liz Reuben would have been if she'd bothered to do research to find out who he was, and then she found out.

Mom came into my room, and she said it wasn't my fault Dale Baker was a dud. "They almost never name schools for interesting people," she said. "The important thing is you found out who he was."

"What if I make up a better Dale Baker?" I asked her.

Mom thought about that, and first she said that wasn't a great idea, because what if Mrs. Coleman looked Dale Baker up too and found out he really wasn't an ax murderer. So I said, "How about if I come up with three different Dale Bakers, so she'll have to know a couple of them are made up, and I can tell her which one is real anyway, but at least she'll have some choices."

"That's a good idea," Mom said. "I bet the Dale Bakers you make up will be more interesting than the real one."

While Mom and I had supper I thought about Dale Bakers and how many interesting ones there could be. Dale Bakers curing cancer and Dale Bakers landing on Mars and Dale Bakers writing great poetry. There could be thousands of great Dale Bakers.

And that was when I had my other great idea. I was making up all these Dale Bakers to get into the gifted and talented program. What if the gifted and talented program had a contest saying whoever came up with the best Dale Baker could be in the gifted and talented program? I'd be the first winner, since it was my idea, but after me, other people could win too, and people who knew they belonged in the gifted and talented program like me could get in that way.

So I told Mom that, and she hugged me and said I had a wonderful imagination, and who were my other Dale Bakers going to be? I asked if they all had to be men, and she said absolutely not, there were a lot of women named Dale too, like Dale Evans, her favorite cowgirl. So I decided that while the real Dale Baker was a guy, my two made up Dale Bakers would be women, exciting women, women a lot more exciting than the real Dale Baker was. Not that women are more exciting than men. But Mrs. Coleman is a woman, so I thought she might like that.

I decided to make one Dale Baker a teacher, just like Mrs. Coleman, only gifted and talented. Just being a teacher didn't seem that exciting to me (when I told Mom that she sighed and said not everybody got to climb Mount Everest) so I made her a schoolteacher a long time ago. That way at least she'd get to wear interesting clothes. I figured I'd have her teach in a one-room schoolhouse, because that might be interesting too.

And then I thought what would be really interesting would be if Dale Baker the schoolteacher did something schoolteachers don't usually get to do, like climb Mount Everest or wrestle a bear. I went with the bear.

I told Mom Dale Baker was going to wrestle a bear, and she said, "That's very exciting. It's too bad we can't actually see it," and that was when I decided to tell the story in a comic book. I'm sending you a copy of the pencil sketch I did for the first page. When I made the actual comic book (I finished it Thursday night), the bear looked a lot more like a bear, but Mom says you'll get the general idea. It was real hard drawing Dale Baker wrestling with the bear, and I don't think I'll get into the gifted and talented program based on my artwork.

I still wanted another Dale Baker who was a woman, and I wanted her to be brave and worthy of having a school named after her, and I came up with the idea that she could be a nurse in World War Two. Mom liked that one too. I thought about writing a poem, but then I decided a song would be even better, only it's been a year since I played the bassoon, so I didn't think I could write the music myself.

"Borrow the tune for 'The Battle Hymn of the Republic,' " Mom said. "That's what Julia Ward Howe did."

So I did too. I'm sending you a copy of "The Ballad of Dale Baker," which I think is an absolutely great song. Mom says just rhyming bayonet and tourniquet should get me into the gifted and talented program, but my favorite part is the line about strife. We just had strife as a vocabulary word, and it made more sense than knife or wife.

I put all the stuff together in a folder, the comic book and the song and the report on the real Dale

Baker and then I made up a "Who Is Dale Baker?" contest sheet, and instead of handing them to Mrs. Coleman like I wanted to do, so I could see her reaction when she went through them, I just left the folder for her in the office yesterday morning. Inside I put a note that only said, "Dear Mrs. Coleman, What do you think? Laurie Levine."

Now after all that work, I have a ton of schoolwork to do, and it's hard to think about it when all I can think about is Mrs. Coleman reading my folder. But Mom says I can be the most gifted and talented person in the world, and if I flunk all my subjects I'll just end up in the stupid and lazy program, and she's probably right.

Love,
Laurie

P.S. Mom says Dale Baker would be real pleased.

It was a bright and sunny morning as the children entered the one room schoolhouse.

Inside, Mrs. Dale Baker, the school's much loved teacher prepared for that day's lessons.

No one suspected that outside the school a mighty grizzly bear lurked

The students were excited by the lessons Mrs Baker was teaching them.

Although the bear was very fat, he was extremely hungry.

Mrs. Baker was such an exciting teacher, no one noticed the bear looking through the window.

The Ballad of Dale Baker
By Laura Diane Levine
(Sung to the tune of "The Battle Hymn of the Republic")

Oh the battlefields of Europe they did drip with bright red blood,
And the people were so grieving that all their tears did flood.
There were soldiers who were stabbed and some soldiers who were shot.
And the sun beat down real hot.

Chorus: Nurse Dale Baker was so brave.
Many lives she did save.
She kept so many from the grave.
Her nursing was so great.

A wounded brave young soldier lay upon the bloodied soil.
With his bayonet and bullets, all the Nazis he did foil.
But now he was a-dying and just heaven lay ahead.
His blood turned all the grass red.

Chorus

Dale Baker saw the soldier and to his hurt side she ran.
She knew that only she could save this brave young soldier man.
She knew that all her training as a brilliant noble nurse
Could keep him from the hearse.

Chorus

She removed the wretched bullet with the boy's own bayonet
And with her uniform, she did make a tourniquet.
With her courage and her knowledge, she saved the young man's life
In the midst of war and strife.

Chorus

The soldier thanked Nurse Baker for saving him that day
And said some future time he was sure he would repay.
"I promise you a reward far better than some jewel.
For you I'll name a school!"

Chorus

Dear Dad,

I'M IN! I'M IN! I'M IN!

I nearly went crazy all day waiting for Mrs. Coleman to say something to me (not that I saw her), and then right before the last bell, there was an announcement on the P.A. that I should report to room 227, which is Mrs. Coleman's room. Kris got real excited then, but I told her not to because Mrs. Coleman might just want to tell me to leave her alone forever and ever, but I couldn't help hoping. So as soon as I could, I ran to room 227, and there was Mrs. Coleman. She said, "I'm glad to see you, Laurie. This folder is truly clever, and if you're still interested in being in the gifted and talented program for next year, I'd be delighted to have you."

Daddy, it was all I could do to keep from jumping up and down. I just said, "Yeah, I'd like that." So then she said, "I liked Dale Baker the nurse the best," which surprised me because I thought she'd really like Dale Baker the teacher the best, or maybe the real boring Dale Baker, and she also said she liked the idea of the Dale Baker contest, and next year the gifted and talented program could work on it together if that was okay with me. I said it was.

Then she said, "I underestimated you, Laurie. There are a lot of different ways of being gifted and talented, and they include imagination, and the willingness to work independently, and good old-fashioned determination, and you have all those qualities, especially the determination." I guess I nodded then. I didn't know what else to do, since I didn't want to praise myself, or even talk about myself, since us gifted and talented people don't do that.

Then Mrs. Coleman asked if she could keep the folder a little while, so she could show it to different people like the principal, and I said yes, absolutely, and I thanked her some more, and flew out of the room. Kris was waiting for me and she'd heard everything, so she hugged me a lot and told me the gifted and talented program would be a hundred times more fun with me in it. Then we got ice-cream cones to celebrate.

Mom was grading term papers when I got in, and I told her what had happened, and she dropped the term papers and jumped up and down. I jumped along with her, even though I'd done a lot of jumping already with Kris. Then Mom said, "We're eating out to celebrate," and then she said, "No, let's have a party on Saturday instead," and then she said, "Let's eat out tonight and have a party on Saturday," so we ate at the Japanese restaurant, where we eat only on incredibly special occasions, and all during supper we talked about who to invite Saturday. We're going to have Kris and Shannon and Jimmy and Joe Malone (Mom says she wants to see them fight over me), and Bill Washington (I don't know if I've mentioned him to you, but he just started school in March and Mom and I figured he'd probably like being invited to a party) and Darin and Jamie (who'd better not scream), and Bruno and Mom and me. Also Darin and Jamie's moms if they want to stick around. Mom said she'd

118

have Bruno come early so he could help with the party, but I think it's to guarantee that he'll be there when Jamie's mom shows up, so Mom can show off Bruno's muscles.

I'm also inviting Victoria Rosamond James, although we don't think she'll get her invitation in time to come. But I'll take pictures during the party, so she can see what all my friends look like.

Mom kept saying how proud of me she was and I'll tell you the truth Dad, I feel pretty proud of me too.

Your gifted and talented
daughter,
Laurie

P.S. We also called up Nana and Gramps and Gran and Grandpa and told all of them, and they said they always knew I was gifted and talented and I should send them copies of the song and comic book and even the boring report so they could show them off. Dale Baker is going to be very famous.

P.P.S. On the way to the Japanese restaurant, Mom and I kept singing *The Ballad of Dale Baker*. It's really an excellent song. Of course, the tune helps.

P.P.P.S. As soon as I told Mom what Mrs. Coleman had said, she asked me if I wanted to call to tell you (the way we called Nana and Gramps and Gran and Grandpa), and the funny thing was, I decided I'd rather write. Maybe because you haven't gotten the letter I sent you yesterday, so it would just be confusing to tell you, but I think it's more that I really love writing you these letters, and I wanted to write you this one too.

April 30

Dear Dad,

Mom and Bruno are running around putting everything together for the party (the guests are due in about half an hour), but I wanted to write you immediately and tell you how much I love the roses you sent.

I don't know what's more beautiful, the roses, or the card. Mom says I can dry the petals and keep them, and the card will go up on my wall, next to the telegram you sent me, so I'll always have both of them forever.

I love you very much.

Love,
Laurie

About the Author

SUSAN BETH PFEFFER is the author of many popular books for young readers including *Truth or Dare*, *The Friendship Pact*, *Turning Thirteen*, and *The Year Without Michael*, which was recently named an ALA Best Book for Young Adults.

Like Liz Reuben, Susan Beth Pfeffer lives and works in Middletown, New York, with her cat Louisa who was the model for the bear pictured in the story.

APPLE®PAPERBACKS

More books you'll love, filled with mystery, adventure, friendship, and fun!

NEW APPLE TITLES

☐ 40284-6	**Christina's Ghost**	Betty Ren Wright	$2.50
☐ 41839-4	**A Ghost in the Window**	Betty Ren Wright	$2.50
☐ 41794-0	**Katie and Those Boys**	Martha Tolles	$2.50
☐ 40565-9	**Secret Agents Four**	Donald J. Sobol	$2.50
☐ 40554-3	**Sixth Grade Sleepover**	Eve Bunting	$2.50
☐ 40419-9	**When the Dolls Woke**	Marjorie Filley Stover	$2.50

BEST SELLING APPLE TITLES

☐ 41042-3	**The Dollhouse Murders**	Betty Ren Wright	$2.50
☐ 42319-3	**The Friendship Pact**	Susan Beth Pfeffer	$2.75
☐ 40755-4	**Ghosts Beneath Our Feet**	Betty Ren Wright	$2.50
☐ 40605-1	**Help! I'm a Prisoner in the Library**	Eth Clifford	$2.50
☐ 40724-4	**Katie's Baby-sitting Job**	Martha Tolles	$2.50
☐ 40494-6	**The Little Gymnast**	Sheila Haigh	$2.50
☐ 40283-8	**Me and Katie (the Pest)**	Ann M. Martin	$2.50
☐ 42316-9	**Nothing's Fair in Fifth Grade**	Barthe DeClements	$2.75
☐ 40607-8	**Secrets in the Attic**	Carol Beach York	$2.50
☐ 40180-7	**Sixth Grade Can Really Kill You**	Barthe DeClements	$2.50
☐ 41118-7	**Tough-Luck Karen**	Johanna Hurwitz	$2.50
☐ 42326-6	**Veronica the Show-off**	Nancy K. Robinson	$2.75
☐ 42374-6	**Who's Reading Darci's Diary?**	Martha Tolles	$2.75

Available wherever you buy books...or use the coupon below.